~~THE ROYAL MONITOR~~

RUNAWAY PRINCE SPOTTED... AT A TEXAS DUDE RANCH!

After days of speculation regarding the whereabouts of Montavia's own heir to the throne, Prince Luc has been spotted in Texas, at a *dude* ranch, of all places! Could our roguish royal possibly be in search of a queen? Maybe... But what worries this reporter most is the pictures the palace has of him actually *riding horses* and *roping cattle*. If this is what one does on a dude ranch, then for a man of such regal lineage to behave like a common farmer is just too much to believe. But pictures don't lie. And will it be only a matter of time before the future king of Montavia is running our beloved country dressed in chaps and a cowboy hat?

Dear Reader,

April is an exciting month for the romance industry because that is when our authors learn whether or not their titles have been nominated for the prestigious RITA® Award sponsored by the Romance Writers of America. As with the Oscars, our authors will find out whether they've actually won in a glamorous evening event that caps off the RWA national conference in July. Of course, all the Silhouette Romance titles this month are already winners to me!

Karen Rose Smith heads up this month's lineup with her tender romance *To Protect and Cherish* (#1810) in which a cowboy-at-heart bachelor becomes a father overnight. *Prince Incognito* (#1811) by Linda Goodnight features another equally unforgettable hero—this one a prince masquerading as an ordinary guy. Nearly everyone accepts his disguise except, of course, our perceptive heroine who is now torn between the dictates of her head…and her heart. Longtime Silhouette Romance author Sharon De Vita returns with *Doctor's Orders* (#1812), in which a single mother who has been badly burned by love discovers a handsome doctor just might have the perfect prescription for her health and longtime happiness. Finally, in Roxann Delaney's *His Queen of Hearts* (#1813), a runaway bride goes from the heat and into the fire when she finds herself holed up in a remote location with her handsome rescuer.

Happy reading!
Sincerely,

Ann Leslie Tuttle
Associate Senior Editor

Please address questions and book requests to:
Silhouette Reader Service
U.S.: 3010 Walden Ave., P.O. Box 1325, Buffalo, NY 14269
Canadian: P.O. Box 609, Fort Erie, Ont. L2A 5X3

PRINCE INCOGNITO
Linda Goodnight

SILHOUETTE *Romance*®

Published by Silhouette Books

America's Publisher of Contemporary Romance

I dedicate this book to Allison Lyons, my editor from
the beginning. You have cheered my successes. You have
steered me in the right direction when I strayed. You have
encouraged me in disappointment. And lest we forget the
really important matters, you introduced me to iced caramel
macchiato. What more could an author want?

 SILHOUETTE BOOKS

ISBN 0-373-19811-6

PRINCE INCOGNITO

Visit Silhouette Books at www.eHarlequin.com

Printed in U.S.A.

Books by Linda Goodnight

Silhouette Romance

For Her Child... #1569
Married in a Month #1682
Her Pregnant Agenda #1690
Saved by the Baby #1709
Rich Man, Poor Bride #1742
The Least Likely Groom #1747
Sometimes When We Kiss #1800
Prince Incognito #1811

LINDA GOODNIGHT

A romantic at heart, Linda Goodnight believes in the traditional values of family and home. Writing books enables her to share her certainty that, with faith and perseverance, love can last forever and happy endings really are possible.

A native of Oklahoma, Linda lives in the country with her husband, Gene, and Mugsy, an adorably obnoxious rat terrier. She and Gene have a blended family of six grown children. An elementary school teacher, she is also a licensed nurse. When time permits, Linda loves to read, watch football and rodeo, and indulge in chocolate. She also enjoys taking long, calorie-burning walks in the nearby woods. Readers can write to her at linda@lindagoodnight.com, or c/o Silhouette Books, 233 Broadway, Suite 1001, New York, NY 10279.

Dear Reader,

Four years ago, Silhouette Romance published my first full-length novel. Right away, I knew I'd found a home for the kind of warm, romantic stories I loved to write as well as read. *Prince Incognito,* my eighth book for this line, continues that tradition, but with a twist.

I thought it would be fun to write a modern Cinderella story complete with handsome prince, a klutzy Cinderella who thought she was an ugly stepsister and a zany fairy godmother like Teddi. I hope you enjoy watching Luc and Carly fall (sometimes quite literally) in love. And I hope you get a chuckle or two out of Teddi.

If you enjoy *Prince Incognito,* please write and let me know. I love hearing from you! Thank you for all the support you've given me since I began writing for Silhouette Romance.

Blessings to you and yours,

Linda Goodnight
www.lindagoodnight.com

Prologue

Carson Benedict stood on the balcony overlooking his domain, the Benedict Guest Ranch. Today was his birthday and, as it turned out, not a particularly happy one.

Teddi, his wacky sister, saw to that. She was pestering him with another of her goofy ideas to make the ranch more prosperous. This one took the cake.

"Look at these ledgers, Carson." She thumped the thick record book and sent six beaded bracelets dancing up and down her slender arms. "We have to do something fast or this guest ranch is going down the tubes."

"We're not doing that bad." They weren't doing that great either.

"Bookings have dropped this summer. Again. Western dude ranches have lost their ambience. The whole romantic mystique of the cowboy is passé. We have to come up with something fresh and modern."

Stifling a groan, Carson stepped through the French double doors into his office, though he knew there was no escaping his sister when she was on a roll. "And you think turning the place into a love nest is going to fix that?"

"You've already ruled out a meditation spa for holistic cleansing," Teddi said, tip-tapping right in behind him with the persistence and energy of a hungry mosquito. "Besides, love is the answer to everyone's problems. Love and aromatherapy."

Carson couldn't hold back a laugh. His baby sister was as New Age as they came, a true disciple of peace and love and healing herbs. With a heavy emphasis on love.

"This is a working ranch, not a bordello." Having guests on the place was bad enough. He sure didn't want a bunch of lovesick greenhorns mooning around.

"Oh, pooh." Teddi tossed her head. A green pyramid-shaped earring, complete with eyeball in the center, flapped against her neck. "That's not what I'm talking about at all. Remember the *Love Boat?* Why not a Love Ranch? A place where lonely singles come to find their one true love."

"No."

"Matching singles is all the rage right now, Carson. It's on the Internet, in churches, colleges. There are even professional matchmaking companies."

"Not here there aren't."

"Okay, then." Teddi tapped the pointy toe of her lime-green shoe with intentional nonchalance. "You win. Let the ranch sink deeper in debt. Let Cousin Arnold buy us out and turn the place into an outlet mall."

She crossed her arms and leaned against the wall. *Tap. Tap. Tap.*

Carson knew that body language. And he also knew his sister would talk incessantly about love until he was ready to jump off the balcony and run screaming through the pasture.

He heaved a sigh strong enough to blow papers off his desk. As uncomfortable as the idea made him, a significant downturn of fortunes for the Benedict Ranch *had* occurred. They did need some kind of advertising gimmick to bring more guests to the ranch. He had hoped the lure of the Old West would do the trick, but Teddi was right. It hadn't.

"Think of something other than a Love Ranch."

"Just because Suzy tossed you over for Brad Holder and his oil wells is no reason to be sour on love."

Carson's blood did a slow boil at the mention of his ex-wife Suzy and the wealthy Brad. Suzy's love had been true and forever—or so she'd said—until his finances had gone south.

"I'll worry about this some other time." He had a budget to wrestle, cattle to cull and a stupid birthday party to endure. "Discussion is closed."

"No." Teddi clamped a hand on each hip, earrings dancing in indignation. For all her flighty ways, she was nearly as stubborn as Carson. "This is my home, too. And keeping it intact affects me as much as it does you. The only way to bring in more guests is to come up with a marketing theme. And what is more appealing than romance?"

"Eating razor blades?"

She narrowed her eyes in speculation. "That's it, isn't it?"

Uh-oh. She had that look. He was about to be whopped upside the head with one of her universal relevance statements. "What's *it?*"

"You, my darling brother—" she slapped a hand on his desk "—are scared."

He frowned. "Of what?"

"That little four-letter word. L-O-V-E. You are so afraid of love that you couldn't convince Romeo and Juliet to go out for free pizza."

"Sure I could." She was starting to make him mad. The very idea that he, a trail-hardened rancher and businessman, was scared of anything put a burr in his saddle. "I just don't want to."

"You could not." Teddi slid onto the edge of his desk, crossed her legs and swung her foot back and forth.

"Could, too."

"Not, not, not." Her foot tapped with each consecutive *not.*

She was taunting him, darn her hide. And it was working. "Look. I had a bad experience, but I am not afraid of love."

"Prove it," she sang in her happy-go-lucky voice.

"How?"

"Do a little matchmaking between our guests."

"No way."

"See," she said smugly. "I knew you couldn't do it."

Carson ground his teeth. Nobody told him he couldn't do something. Not even his flibbertigibbet sister. "Wanna bet?"

"You won't do it."

"I said I would."

"Okay, then. I'll bet that you cannot get the next two single guests to fall in love."

He stuck his nose in her face. "And if I do?"

"I will not say another word about a Love Ranch. But if you lose, I get to rename the ranch and send out the ads."

He felt a smile coming on. "You've got yourself a bet."

Teddi exploded off the desk and into his arms. She almost knocked all six foot two of him onto his jean-clad backside. "Oh, this is perfect. I'll even help you."

"Whoa, wait a minute." What had he gotten himself into? "Why would you help me?"

"Because once you see how powerful love is, you'll be hooked and you'll want us to become the Love County Love Ranch."

Carson was appalled. "No way. You said you'd drop the subject."

"I will." She gave him a sly glance. "If you still want me to. But first you have to make that match." She danced around the office, and Carson knew the wobbly wheels inside her head were in full motion. "We have an absolute hunk of a guy here already."

Carson stiffened. "If you mean Luc Gardner, he is off-limits."

For once Teddi stood still, pinning him with a curious gaze. "He's single, isn't he?"

Yes, he was single and a lot more that a woman would appreciate, but Carson had promised to shelter his royal friend and give him a summer of privacy, not find him a wife. Lucky for him, Teddi had been away contemplating the mysteries of the universe the last time Luc had been to Oklahoma.

"Not Luc," he repeated.

"Has to be. He's the first single guy, and that was the bet."

At the sound of a car door, Teddi rushed to the window and peeked through the gauzy curtain. She turned with a flourish and clapped her hands. "And there is a perfectly acceptable young woman—a little tacky-looking maybe but still a female—arriving down below right this minute."

She sailed to him, kissed him on the cheek and rushed to the door, flinging it open with such exuberance Carson flinched.

"I'll just run down and make her welcome." She started out the door, then stopped, turned and pointed a finger at him. "You made a bet, Carson. You can't renege. It would be very bad karma and upset the cosmic balance of this ranch."

The cosmic balance, as Carson saw it, was already in bad shape. But he'd never reneged on a bet in his life. Much as he wished he'd kept his mouth shut, his word was his bond. He was about to push his royal college buddy down the road to romance.

He stifled a shudder.

Anything to keep from renaming his ancestral home the Love County Love Ranch.

Chapter One

*E*xiled.

With a huge groan of dismay, Carly Carpenter popped the trunk on her green Camry and dragged out the one bag she always carried on assignment along with her tape recorder and a laptop. On second thought, she shoved the recorder back inside. Who in Maribella, Oklahoma, would be worth taping?

She stared up at the sprawling three-story turn-of-the-century guest ranch located in the middle of ten thousand acres of nothing and wondered why on earth her sister, Meg, had picked this spot for her exile. Oh, she had said it wasn't an exile, but Carly knew better. Meg's husband, Eric, owner and head detective at Wright Stuff Investigations, would have fired her on the spot had Meg not sent her somewhere to hide until the smoke cleared.

"One little mistake," she muttered. The night had been dark. She hadn't even seen the flowerpot. Having finally caught Sam Kensel out of his wheelchair and neck brace, she'd been too excited to notice the open window. After all, the guy was suing his workplace for millions, claiming total disability from an on-the-job injury. And then there he was, big as Dallas, pumping hundred-pound weights like Arnold Schwarzenegger, sans neck brace, sans wheelchair and without a trace of pain on his face. She'd tiptoed closer, grappled for her camera and stumbled over the azaleas, through the open window and right into Sam Kensel's private den.

Sure, the investigation was completely blown after seven long months of tailing, spying and secret recordings. Sure, her brother-in-law had lost a boatload of money and a healthy slice of his reputation as the best in the west. But was it her fault someone stuck a blasted azalea pot under the window? And wasn't the embarrassment of being Carly the Klutz punishment enough?

"Sheesh." She slammed the trunk only to discover the sleeve of her oversize shirt-jacket was caught inside. She yanked hard. Then heard a rip. Sadly she looked down at the shirt borrowed from her dad. She preferred baggy, oversize clothes, and his fit the bill. They made her feel shorter, instead of a gawky, lanky five-foot-nine tower of hair and arms and legs.

Not that she cared about such things as fashion. Not Carly Carpenter. She was a private investigator—or wanted to be—with no time for fancy fingernails or frilly clothes or afternoons spent in beauty parlors. Each morning she pulled her thick brunette hair into a wad at the nape of her neck with a rubber band, shoved one of those teeth-clamp thingies in it and hoped the mess stayed in place. It never did.

She shrugged, and the aforementioned hair tumbled forward. Big deal. Let the stuff fall.

Her job was her life, and she was good at it, though her brother-in-law and half of Dallas would argue that point. Somehow she had to get back into their good graces. Breaking a case was the best way, but where would she find a case worth investigating here amidst miles and miles of cows and grass? Sheesh, she could just see the headlines now. P.I. Busts Mayor for Midnight Cow Tipping.

"Take a vacation. Rest up. Recharge your engines," her sister had said, handing her the brochure for the Benedict Guest Ranch less than two hours' drive from Dallas. "This place is a real ranch complete with cowboys and horses and cattle drives. You're gonna love it."

When she'd tried to argue that she really wanted to be investigating something, Meg had held up a commanding hand.

"I'm trying to save your job, sis. You have a paid vacation coming. Go. Let things around here cool off for a while. Give me time to work a little magic on Eric."

And so here she was, with one ripped shirtsleeve and a very bruised ego, exiled to the Benedict Guest Ranch for an undetermined amount of time. Meg had said not to come home until she called for her. Now there was a scary thought.

Refusing to let her shoulders slump, she approached

the large wraparound porch. The three-story house was right out of a John Wayne movie.

A movement from above drew her attention. On the upper balcony a curtain twitched and a face briefly appeared.

Her private investigator's curiosity leaped to the fore. Who would be the least bit interested in her arrival?

She shrugged, and the torn overblouse slid down on one shoulder. Absolutely nobody. She hiked up the sleeve, set down her bags, pushed on the brass door handle and entered a massive foyer. The antique portrait of a sour-faced man with slicked-down hair and his equally sour-faced wife glowered down from the Victorian rose wallpaper. Why would anyone hang such an unwelcoming picture in the entryway?

From the corner of her eye she caught sight of a large open area to the right complete with a horseshoe-shaped reception desk.

Still staring at the ugly couple, she stepped sideways directly into the chest wall of a tall, very well-built man. An expensive-smelling man. She lifted her gaze past the pearlized shirt buttons, over the classic Western yoke and into a face straight out of Greek mythology. Breath lodged in her throat.

"Hello." He gave her a smile that said he was very accustomed to having women fall at his feet. What he didn't know was that Carly fell at everybody's feet, handsome or not.

Fumbling for words while trying to close her fly-trap mouth, she managed, however reluctantly, to push herself away from the hard, muscular chest.

"I am so sorry. I'm so clumsy at times, but that picture…" She glanced over her shoulder and grimaced.

He removed his hat and Carly's mouth went dry. Oh, man.

The gorgeous cowboy had bad-boy hair, the kind that drove women wild. Unruly, curly and a tad too long, the dark blond locks were a fantasy created for a woman's fingers.

"If I understand correctly, those were the original Benedicts who built this house. And the photograph was taken on their wedding day."

Carly forced her gaze back to the ugly picture with a stern reminder that she was not interested in men, no matter how hunky and hot. "Not exactly a match made in heaven, was it?"

The cowboy-god laughed. "According to the family, they were actually very happy together."

"Takes all kinds, I suppose. But it does make you wonder about the rest of the Benedicts."

"Actually the hospitality is exceptional."

"Thank goodness. Those are not faces I would enjoy seeing over the dinner table every night."

"So you are a guest here, too. No?"

The odd turn of phrase elevated Carly's investigative antennae. Did she detect a wisp of an accent? She checked him out one more time. He *looked* like a cowboy. But then this *was* a dude ranch. Anybody could buy a hat and boots.

"I'll be staying for a while." She thought of herself as more of a prisoner than a guest.

"And you are not too happy about that?"

"Long story." A humiliation she did not care to share with anyone, certainly not a gorgeous man who exuded class. She bent to retrieve her bags, but the cowboy was too quick for her.

"Allow me."

Carly gawked at the perfectly vee'd back moving away from her, a bag under each arm. Since when did cowboys talk so cultured? And walk with the erect bearing of a soldier and the smooth grace of someone born to privilege? Cowboys slouched. Or strutted.

But not so this guy. She had a quick vision of servants and valets and bellboys rushing to accommodate his every wish. And women lined up to ride in his fancy Italian car.

She didn't care if he wore spurs and chaps and shouted, "Yee-haw." This fella was no more a cowboy than she was. An aristocrat, no doubt, with blood bluer than his eyes. The smell of money and privilege teased her senses as much as his designer cologne.

She turned up her nose. Guys like this thought they were so hot. He'd probably expect her to fall all over him, flirt and generally make a nuisance of herself. And maybe, just maybe, he'd drop a crumb in her lap.

Carly didn't worry about that in the least. She might fall on him, but not out of attraction. Not Carly. She'd been ignored by the best and dumped by the worst. No big deal.

Hiking her torn shirtsleeve, she followed the man across the gleaming oak floor to the horseshoe reception desk. A mouse of a woman awaited her.

"I'm Carly Carpenter."

The skinny woman whose name badge read Macy shoved a pair of enormous black plastic glasses toward her nose.

"Of course, ma'am. We were expecting you." She pushed a form across the desk. "Please sign this and you'll be set to go. The second floor is our guest area. You are in room number—" she squinted at the key in her hand "—three. Just down the hall past Mr. Gardner. I see the two of you have already met."

"I guess you could say we bumped into each other."

Lowering Carly's bags to the floor, the man flashed his million-dollar smile. Carly decided not to notice. She was off men like feathers off a plucked chicken. Permanently.

He extended a well-groomed hand. No dirt under those fingernails. "I am Luc Gardner."

Carly placed her hand in his. She, with hands long enough to have been a concert pianist, was dwarfed by a blond god in cowboy boots. An interesting sizzle of awareness shimmied up one arm. That would not do at all.

"And I am Carly Carpenter, klutz deluxe. Look out for the shine on those boots. If I'm anywhere near, they'll be toast."

He smiled, and somewhere an orthodontist rejoiced. "Toast? As in breakfast?"

Carly blinked twice. What kind of guy didn't understand American idioms?

A lightbulb came on inside her head.

"You're not American."

"As you would say, busted." The corners of his ocean-blue eyes crinkled, but she detected a flicker of reservation. Had he not wanted her to realize the obvious?

But Carly had no opportunity to probe further. An elf of a woman bounded down the staircase to the right, long stained-glass pyramids swinging from her earlobes, brown curly hair flying around her shoulders.

"Hi, Luc. So sweet of you to play bellhop. I don't know where those ranch hands have gotten off to." A fleeting pucker came and went, replaced by an impish grin. "Out playing cowboy, I imagine." Then she stuck out a hand toward Carly. "I'm Teddi Benedict and you must be Carly Carpenter." Before Carly had a chance to answer, Teddi whipped around toward the mousy little receptionist. "Macy, did you tell them about tonight's barbecue for Carson and the trail ride in the morning?"

Carly's head swirled as fast as the woman's colorful gypsylike skirts. This must be one of *the* Benedicts.

"Today's my brother's birthday." Teddi flashed a grin. "And we're celebrating with a bash at seven o'clock. A great way to get acquainted with the staff and the other guests."

"Oh. Well. That's…good." Just what Carly didn't need. To have to make nice when all she wanted to do was go up to her room and fall into a hot bath and a long depression.

"Here you go." Teddi shoved a piece of paper that looked like something of a schedule into Carly's hand. "Everything you need to know is right there. Now, Luc, sweetie, would you mind carrying Carly's bags up the stairs for her?"

No one had carried anything for Carly since Harold Watersnout in the fourth grade. And he'd only done it then so she'd teach him to whistle through his front teeth.

But the man with the designer smile, the continental bearing and athletic body inclined his head and hoisted her bag and laptop one more time. "It would be my pleasure."

An exaggeration, no doubt, but Carly gave him points for good manners. Carrying a guest's suitcase couldn't be a normal occurrence for a Greek god.

Investigator's curiosity—at least that's what she told herself—drove her to watch him. Long, athletic, jean-clad legs carried Mr. Golden Gorgeous up the staircase.

She tugged at the neck of her ripped shirt.

My goodness, it was warm in here.

Everything about her new acquaintance screamed wealth and privilege, the kind of man who normally left her as cold as a tile floor on Christmas morning.

But something about the pseudo cowboy intrigued her. Purely detective's instinct.

What was a man like Luc Gardner doing on an Oklahoma dude ranch?

She shrugged once more to hike the torn sleeve back into place. She was a detective. She'd find out soon enough.

As she clumped up the rather narrow staircase behind him, Carly did her best not to drool. The man was scary handsome. Fairy-tale handsome. And Carly was a realist who did not believe in fairy tales.

"Room three, isn't it?" He paused outside the door a few feet down the gleaming wood-floor hallway.

"Yes."

He extended his hand. She stared at him like an idiot for a full minute before understanding that he wanted to unlock the door for her.

Flattered, she handed him the key. "I'm perfectly capable of opening the door for myself."

"And my mother would be appalled if I allowed it."

She smiled. "I like your mother."

He returned the smile, and Carly prayed her eyes wouldn't cross from the brilliance. "As do I."

He inserted the key, then stood back, allowing Carly to enter first.

After setting her bag on the floor, he placed the laptop on the small table next to the bed.

"Someone left you a newspaper." He picked the thing up as he would a dead mouse.

She grimaced. Hadn't this very Dallas newspaper carried the story of her arrest for breaking and entering? Sheesh. She'd *fallen* and entered, and the only thing she'd come close to breaking was her own neck.

"The last thing I want to see while I'm here is a newspaper."

Luc Gardner dropped the *Dallas Daily Mirror* into the trash can. "I feel exactly the same."

"You don't like the media?" She went to a small round table to smell the flowers and finger the fruit. Her shirt-sleeve slid down again. This time she gave up and left it.

"Not particularly. Prying into someone else's private life for gain is not my idea of a worthy occupation."

Ouch. "Really?"

If he thought reporters were nosy, what would he think of a private investigator? Better lie low with this guy and keep her career goals to herself.

Carly polished a shiny red apple on the tail of her shirt and tried not to watch him from the corner of her eye. He really was gorgeous. "How long have you been here?"

He crossed his arms and leaned against the open door facing her. "Two days."

"Planning to stay long?" Rats. Where had that come from?

"As long as it takes."

Interesting answer. "To do what?"

"Get to know you, of course."

Carly laughed. She knew her shortcomings. Guys liked her. They confided in her. Asked her advice. Treated her like a sister or a best friend. A few even dated her. But no one tossed compliments to Carly the Klutz.

Certainly not guys like this one.

So why had he?

Chapter Two

Luc unlocked the door to his own room and went inside, tossing the white cowboy hat onto the bed. He was still thinking about the latest guest to arrive at the Benedict Ranch.

She amused him, did Miss Carly Carpenter, with her quick wit and baggy attire. Not the usual woman of his acquaintance, but that was the appeal, he thought. She hadn't simpered and fawned over him.

Probably because, to his enormous relief, she had no idea who he was. For once he was in a place where not one person—other than his old college mate, Carson Benedict—had even a hint of who he was.

Never in his life had he been out of the limelight, though he'd lived in the shadow of his brother for most of the time. But since Philippe's death, the European paparazzi had turned into blood-sucking leeches, draining every moment of peace from his life. The American press, while fascinated by him during his brief time at university, had yet to discover his presence this trip.

He could thank Carson for that. His friend had graciously agreed to protect his privacy and in effect hide him out for this last summer. His summer of decision.

He rubbed at the little knot of tension in his neck and went to the computer on the small desk next to the window. Though he wasn't picky about accommodations, the room was pleasant and sparkling clean.

Knotty-pine walls surrounded an ample-size bed covered in a colorful red-and-blue Americana quilt. A large area rug was beneath his feet, and a small bathroom opened off to one side. He knew from conversations with Carson that the baths had been added when the ranch had opened its doors to visitors.

He felt for his old friend, a quiet loner of a man who must be constantly annoyed to have strangers running about his land. Carson had been as much a misfit at Princeton as he, though for far different reasons. They had become such good friends because they'd both sought solitude and peace where there was none.

Flipping open the lid of the laptop, Luc typed in his password and opened his e-mail, checking for word from the palace in Montavia. He'd promised his father, King Alexandre, that he would be in frequent communication should a crisis arise and he needed to return home—something he didn't want to do anytime soon. Oh, he loved his country and the warm, gentle people living there, just as he felt the strong call of duty upon his life.

But when he'd come to Oklahoma on spring break with Carson during that one year Father had allowed him to attend a foreign university, he'd been free of the conventions and diplomacy that ruled his life—or tried to.

That one glorious year when he'd fallen in love with a country other than his own and had completed a degree in resort development. A degree that he had hoped to use as a means of strengthening his small country's role in the global economy, though the press had mocked his interest as an excuse for the lesser prince to play.

"The playboy prince," they'd called him. And though he was much less the playboy than the tabloids had indicated, he'd done his share of playing. He made no excuses for enjoying life. Race cars, fast horses, ski competitions. He'd gloried in them all.

Then, only days before his twenty-seventh birthday, Philippe, crown prince of Montavia, had died. His brother, his best friend, killed during Christmas vacation while they'd skied in the Alps.

With great effort Luc closed off the thought of that day, of the flash of red on white snow, the utter silence that had come after and the terrible knowledge of his own culpability.

Then he, Luc Jardine, the playboy prince, the second son, had become the heir apparent. And life had never been the same again.

He'd been reared to serve, reared even to reign should that become necessary, but no one had ever believed anything would happen to Philippe. Mother and Father had trained both sons in government, but Luc had resisted more than he'd cooperated. He had skipped as many international summits and state dinners as he'd attended.

Philippe, so serious and intellectual, had never taken his responsibility lightly, not the way Luc had. Philippe would have made a strong and able king, just as he'd been a steadfast and loving brother. Even now Luc's heart bled with missing the best friend he would ever know.

He rubbed a hand over his suddenly misty eyes. Philippe had been the right man for the throne. Luc, the playboy prince, felt he never would be.

And that was where the indecision lay. Could he rule?

When Father had shipped him off to the military shortly following Philippe's death, Luc had been too stunned and grief-stricken to argue. The experience had strengthened his character, taken the edge off his wildness and made him a better man, but had it made him a king? He didn't know. And until he did, he could not accept the crown from his father.

A tiny computer voice announced that he had mail. The post was from his sister and only remaining sibling. His fingers tightened as he highlighted the e-mail. If Anastasia found out where he was, word would spread all over Europe—and America—by morning. Anastasia, much as he adored her, had never kept a secret in her life.

Luc! the post screamed. Wherever are you? Count Broussard is in an absolute frenzy over your disappearance.

Luc frowned at the screen. Count Broussard, royal counselor and personal advisor to the crown prince, was the main reason he had eluded his entourage of bodyguards and come to America.

From the time he was a boy and more so since Philippe's death, the count had hovered over Luc like an overprotective mother—or a vulture. Luc could make no decision, go nowhere, do nothing without Broussard's input—and frequently his disapproval. Nothing Luc did was right in the eyes of the royal advisor. Even his father had noticed and agreed with Luc's decision to spend some time alone, away from the pressures of the palace, the press and the count.

Shaking off a sense of unease, Luc continued reading.

That wicked old Peter won't tell me anything, and Father only shoos me away like some annoying insect. I will surely perish if I do not hear from you soon.

Anastasia's flare for the dramatic triggered a smile. Next to Broussard, his little sister was the last person who could know his whereabouts. She loved to talk, especially to the Montavian press.

The next post was from his valet and confidant, the dependable Peter. Newsy and warm and full of humor, the post made Luc wish for home. One paragraph, written to bedevil, reminded Luc that Lady Priscilla was still miffed at him. He laughed aloud and dashed off an answering note.

Lady Priscilla, Count Broussard's daughter, was a constant source of agitation and teasing between the two men. Luc's father, as well as the count, would like nothing better than to see a match between the crown prince and Lady Priscilla. Time was passing. The unspoken pressure to marry an appropriate woman and produce a male heir grew stronger all the time.

He splayed four fingers through his unruly hair. He had no desire to settle down with one woman.

His thoughts went to the endearing bag lady he'd met in the lobby, Carly Carpenter. She was nothing at all like Lady Priscilla. But he had a suspicion that beneath the oversize shirt, floppy skirt and hiking boots there could be a lovely woman.

He shook his head, smiling. Perhaps not. Either way, his interest had been piqued. He had enjoyed the contradiction of her snappy attitude and bag-lady looks with her sexy drawl and full, lush mouth. A man could fantasize about a mouth like that.

Suddenly he was looking forward to Carson's birthday party.

Carly had tried resting in her cute country-style room, but she wasn't tired. She was, however, fighting an annoying bout of depression. She, who did not believe in allowing her emotions to run her life and who hadn't even cried over her breakup last month with Lester, was in danger of becoming morose.

Lester the Molester, as she'd called him after threatening to amputate both his hands if he didn't keep them out from under her skirt, was not worth her tears. Her career, however, was.

Sad to think that her job had been her life and now she didn't even have a job. Maybe she'd never work again. Maybe she was washed up at the age of twenty-eight and would spend the rest of her life living in boxes behind Burger King, investigating half-eaten sandwiches and cigarette butts.

No, her sweet sister, Meg, wouldn't let that happen. She'd wine and dine good old Eric, give him a few of her pretty pouts and hot looks, and soon enough Carly would be back to work.

Maybe. And then again, maybe Meg's charm wouldn't work this time.

Carly snapped off Court TV and looked at her watch. Nearly time for the evening's entertainment, a diversion at least from her worries. She hitched her camera strap over one shoulder and headed down the hall toward the stairs.

Nearing room six—the drugstore cowboy's room— she paused. Would Luc Gardner attend the barbecue?

Before she could think better of it, Carly lifted a hand to knock and ask. Hearing a *tap, tap, tap*, she hesitated and then decided against disturbing him. Silly idea anyway. Even if she was only being friendly.

The tapping continued, and true to her nosy inclinations, she pressed an ear to the door. Not that she was interested in him otherwise. But her instinct had been titillated by that accent of his and she aimed to find out more about him. What was he doing in there? Typing? Doing computer work? Was he a workaholic businessman who couldn't leave his job behind even for a vacation?

Sheesh. She was a fine one to ask that.

Suddenly the tapping stopped and chair rollers clattered against the wood floor. Before she could be caught snooping, Carly rushed down the curving stairs. On the very last step she twisted her ankle and was forced to hop on one foot across the wide wraparound veranda.

Though she had yet to learn her way around the ranch, it didn't take a detective to follow the scent of mesquite smoke. Stomach growling, ankle throbbing, she limped down a red brick walkway that snaked around the house to the wide backyard.

A recreation area of sorts sprawled out in all directions. She spotted a swimming pool at one end, horseshoe pits and a volleyball net at the other. In the center was a smoker the size of a tanker and enough men in cowboy hats to fill Dodge City. The women were outnumbered ten to one.

She should have been giddy at the opportunity to hang out with so many of the opposite sex. But not Carly. She was resigned to the hideous truth that men did not find her attractive. There were women with beauty and there were those with brains. She would never fit into the first category, so she darn well intended to claim the latter.

"Carly." The effusive welcome committee, Teddi Benedict, danced toward her. Carly had visions of gypsies circling a campfire, tambourines a-jingle. "Come and meet everyone. Supper is almost ready."

Over the next few minutes Carly was pulled from cowboy to cowboy for introductions. Head swimming with names like Slim and Dirk and Heck, her thoughts went to the one cowboy who looked more like Rodeo Drive than a real rodeo.

She glanced around. No sign of the intriguing Luc.

Teddi led her toward an enormous shade tree where a man and a small boy stood apart from the crowd. The ugliest dog on the planet sat between the two, never taking his spooky but adoring eyes off the child.

"And this," Teddi announced with glee, "is my big brother, Carson, the birthday boy."

"Happy birthday, Mr. Benedict," Carly said. "Thank you for inviting me to your party."

A tall, dark cowboy with black eyes and a blacker expression glowered at her.

"Welcome to Benedict Ranch," he growled.

Carly blinked. Mr. Carson Benedict, birthday or not, was not a happy camper.

"And this little man is Gavin," Teddi went on, indicating a smaller spitting image of Carson Benedict, complete with boots and hat and a belt buckle that covered his entire belly.

The darling boy stuck out a hand with solemn politeness. "Welcome to Benedict Ranch."

Charmed, Carly bent from her considerable height to eye level with the child.

"Why, thank you, sir. I take it you are the owner of this fine ranch."

The child beamed, and the real owner even managed a grudging reply. "Gavin will own this spread someday no matter what I have to do."

Thinking his was an oddly defensive remark to a total stranger, Carly mumbled something and moved away. Carson Benedict was about as friendly as a rattlesnake. And he didn't seem the least bit thrilled to have all these guests on his land, though he was the owner and must have the ultimate say in what happened here. And if he was in a celebratory mood for his birthday, she didn't want to be around when he was ticked off.

Weird.

"Pay no mind to Carson," Teddi said, catching up to her. "His bad attitude is just an act."

"Well, he's good at it. Has he ever thought of a career on the stage?"

Teddi's musical laughter rang out. "Too busy worrying about this place, I think."

No doubt operating such an establishment did require a great deal of work.

"How many guests can you accommodate?" she asked, taking in green pastures and barbwire fences that spread as far as the eye could see.

"Thirty at the most." Teddi Benedict was never still, and in the evening sun her brown hair glinted with red highlights. "Other than the house, we have two bunkhouses—one for guests and one for the cowboys."

"Ah. A real working ranch, then? Just like in the brochure."

"Absolutely. If you want to ride out and work with the hands, you can do that. Or you can go for the planned events, trail rides, whatever you want." Teddi did one of her mercurial shifts, hazel eyes dancing. "This place is perfect for the single female. You are single, aren't you?"

"Uh…yeah." Permanently.

As if Carly's unattached status was something to celebrate, Teddi clapped her small hands and nearly did a jitterbug.

"Wonderful, Carly. You are surrounded by men." She swept a hand toward the gaggle of cowboys who now held paper plates and chowed down on pork ribs. "Find one. Have a romantic holiday. Maybe even discover your one true love. This place can make it happen."

Carly held up a hand to stop the tirade. "Thanks, but no thanks. Romance is the last thing on my mind."

And would likely stay that way forever. She didn't need a man; she needed to successfully investigate something and prove to her brother-in-law that she really could solve a case without screwing up.

As if that was going to happen out here in cowville.

At that moment Luc Gardner came strolling down the brick walk, thumbs in his belt loops, looking mouthwateringly delicious. Carly forgot what she was saying.

"Luc!" Teddi gushed, jewelry clanking like a ghost in chains. "I'm so glad you decided to join us."

"The scent of Western barbecue could drive a man to madness."

"Exactly the result we were going for. Tell you what. You met Carly earlier, right?"

Luc turned those Mediterranean-blue eyes on Carly and smiled. "Lovely seeing you again, Carly."

"Yes, lovely," she mumbled weakly. She was salivating, but it had nothing to do with the spicy barbecue.

Before she could make a bigger fool of herself, Teddi stepped in. "So, Luc, sweetie, will you be Carly's dinner partner tonight and help her get acquainted?"

"That isn't necessary." Now that she'd found her voice and had shaken off the annoying attack of weak knees, Carly was embarrassed at Teddi's machinations.

"It would be my pleasure," Luc replied over her protestations.

Teddi squeezed his bicep, setting her bracelets a-jingle. "Oh, I just knew you would. You are such a sweetheart. If y'all will excuse me, I really should go say hello to the new family from Ohio."

Like a will-o'-the-wisp, she danced away, leaving Carly alone with Luc. How embarrassing. And how awful for Luc to be put on the spot this way. All her life her family had played matchmaker, dumping her on unsuspecting guys—and it never worked out.

"Really, Luc," she said, liking the way his name rolled off her tongue but not particularly fond of her sudden propensity for stuttering, "I can fend for myself."

"But I am alone here, too. I would enjoy sharing dinner with you." He made it sound as though they were dining on caviar and champagne at the Ritz. "That is, if you are in agreement."

Agreement? Ecstasy was more like it. Not because he was far more handsome than any man here. And not because his accent made her stomach flutter. But because she wanted to know why a man like him was here, alone, on an Oklahoma dude ranch a million miles from nowhere. That was all. Mere P.I.'s curiosity.

"You do not mind, however, if I greet our host first?" Luc went on. "Would you care to accompany me?"

After their initial meeting, she had no desire to play chummy with the dour rancher.

She grimaced. "I'll pass."

Luc looked at her quizzically. "Have the two of you met?"

"A few moments ago. And I have to tell you, the birthday boy isn't the friendliest host around."

"Carson?" Luc's blue gaze flickered to the rancher now sitting at a picnic table with the small boy. The incredibly ugly blue-eyed dog sat on the bench, too. "Carson is all right. A bit too private to run a bed-and-breakfast but a good man nonetheless."

His answer surprised her. How would a guest make that kind of evaluation in two days' time?

"Then why don't you go say hello while I get us a couple glasses of iced tea." She pointed to a table covered in red-checkered vinyl. "I'll meet you under that tree over there."

Like a king honoring his subjects, Luc inclined his golden head. "Excellent idea."

As Luc strolled away, Carly headed for a shaded area where Macy, the ranch's receptionist, manned a spigoted container of sweet tea. Behind Macy an angelic-looking toddler sat on a quilt, gnawing a banana.

"Who's the cutie-pie?" Carly asked.

Mousy Macy, as Carly had secretly termed her, lit up like the night sky on the Fourth of July. "That's Hanna, my little girl. She's two."

The child, all blue eyes and curly blond hair, waved a chubby hand at Carly. "Hi."

"Hi, yourself," Carly said before glancing back to Macy. "She's adorable."

Macy filled a large plastic cup with tea and handed it to Carly. Her voice was soft and shy. "Thank you. I think so, too."

Once upon a time when she had believed in fairy tales, Carly had thought about having kids. But that was before she'd grown up and discovered she was better at poking around in other people's business than in forming lasting relationships.

After collecting the drinks, Carly headed for the shade tree and sat down. Sipping at the icy, sweet beverage, her attention drifted to Luc and the unfriendly rancher. Her curiosity hitched a notch. In Luc's company, the grumpy Carson was laughing and relaxed. He clapped a hand on Luc's shoulder as if they were old friends.

How would a remote Oklahoma rancher become acquainted with someone who oozed European class? Interesting question that Carly intended to answer.

"So," Carly said a short time later as she sat across the table from Luc stabbing a fork into beef chunks loaded with spicy-hot barbecue sauce. "Are you and Mr. Benedict old friends?"

Nothing like going straight to the source with a direct question. She was much more adept at interviewing than conversation anyway. Concentrating on business would erase the discomfort of being thrust upon Luc like some wallflower at the junior prom.

Luc hesitated, lifting his napkin.

If possible, he looked even more fairy-tale handsome tonight in a chambray shirt that turned his eyes to a rhapsody in blue. And if that wasn't enough to make her drool like a sick dog, he'd rolled back the sleeves to reveal muscled forearms that looked strong enough to take on anything. So interesting. Both muscles and manners in one stunning body.

To make matters worse—or better, depending on one's outlook—he had removed the white cowboy hat. Carly had nearly choked on her barbecue. That wild bad-boy hair, like some sexy movie star or European racer, wreaked havoc with her imagination.

"Carson and I attended the same university for a short time," he said. "So when I decided to vacation in the American West, I contacted him."

Well, that explained it. Shoot.

Disappointed, she stabbed another beef chunk and poked it in her mouth. She'd hoped for a more exciting reason for a man like Luc to vacation at a remote dude ranch in Oklahoma instead of on the sunny shores of Spain.

She chewed and swallowed, savoring the tender beef. "Somebody around here has turned barbecue into an art form."

"That would be Carson's specialty. I remember when he invited me here years ago. He could hardly wait until I had tasted the family recipe. It is exquisite, no?"

There was that accent again, richer, warmer.

"You never did say where you are from."

"No, I never did." He smiled to soften the evasive reply, but Carly didn't miss the diversion. Her antennae shot, happily, back up.

"Your accent is charming," she said. "Is it French?"

She was prying but hoped Luc accepted the question as casual dinner conversation.

"You have a good ear," he said. "Perhaps you speak *français?*"

"Oui." She racked her brain to tell him that she had learned basic French in high school. *"J'ai appris dans le lycée."*

His face, already too gorgeous for words, lit up in pleasant surprise. *"Votre accent est tout à fait passable."*

Carly grinned at his compliment about her French accent and searched for the phrase to tell him not to tease her for sounding like a Texan.

"Ne taquinez pas. Je suis une Texan."

Luc leaned back from the table and lay his fork aside to study her intently. "I am impressed, *mademoiselle. ¿Usted habla español?"*

Carly's brain whirled to keep pace, but she was determined to be his mental equal. She might not be a beauty, but she had smarts.

She pointed her fork at him. "No fair jumping to Spanish without warning. But *si,* I do know some Spanish, though mine is mostly street language from living and working among the Hispanic folks in Dallas."

"Quizás usted puede enseñarme."

The pleasure of doing mental gymnastics with an intelligent man stirred Carly's blood. Most men of her acquaintance were intimidated by her quick mind, but with Luc the situation was just the opposite. And tons of fun.

"I would be delighted to share the street language I know—if you think you can stand it."

"I look forward to your expertise. *Möglicherweise sprechen Sie auch Deutsches?*"

Darn. She'd used up her repertoire of foreign languages.

She shook her head. One lock of hair came loose and flopped into her face. She blew it back. "You lost me there. What was that? German?"

"Ja." He took up his fork and knife again, slicing his beef as if it was filet mignon.

"How many languages do you speak anyway?"

She watched him eat, noting that though he enjoyed his food with manly gusto, he ate with a finesse not found on most ranches. Muscles, manners and an amazing mind. Who was this guy?

"Six fluently. And you?"

"Six? Now it's my turn to be impressed. Sadly you have heard my entire litany of languages. Where did you learn to speak so many?"

Luc's expression remained friendly, but his smile tightened. Interesting. They had both enjoyed their game of intellectual table tennis, so why the sudden tension?

"School. Travel." He gestured with his fork. "You know."

No, she didn't know, but as a detective—junior though she might be—she recognized the carefully chosen words that answered without answering.

"French, German, Spanish, English and what else?" she pressed with her most charming smile. Was he being intentionally obtuse or had a couple of years of prying information out of reluctant interviewees made her overly suspicious?

"Italian and Chinese."

"I'm out of the game on both of those. Isn't Chinese incredibly difficult?"

"It is, but in my—" he hesitated slightly, and her radar went crazy "—family business we found Chinese to be an important asset."

"So your family is in international business?"

"More…public relations, you might say."

"But on an international scale?"

"The world has become a global economy. Every large business is now on an international scale, is it not?"

Ah, now she was a getting somewhere. He was in some kind of public-relations business that had been in the family for generations and had gone international. No wonder he reeked of money and privilege—and spoke more languages than the United Nations.

"And what of you, Carly?" he asked. "What do you do in Texas?"

Think fast, Carly. You're about to get in over your head.

"My degree is in marketing." Which was true. Never mind that she'd nearly gone loco during the single year she'd worked in the field. She and the nine-to-five suit set weren't exactly a match made in heaven.

"Do you enjoy it?"

Hated it.

She shrugged and felt her sleeve slide south. "Some days are diamond and some are stone."

Lately the stones had been winning.

Luc's glorious eyebrows knit together in a question. "Pardon?"

"Oh." She flapped one hand at him. "It's just a job, like any other. I take the good with the bad." She had to find a way out of this conversation quick. "My life is boring. Yours, on the other hand, with all that international travel must be fascinating. Tell me about your country."

Hopefully her attempt to keep Luc talking about himself was subtle enough to catch him off guard. She was usually good at sneaky interrogation.

His already dreamy eyes took on an even dreamier expression. Wherever he lived was a place he loved.

"Ours," he said, "is a small but lush and picturesque country surrounded by mountains, dotted with pristine villages and peopled by a warm and friendly citizenry."

Sunlight shafting through the trees glinted off his bad-boy hair. Carly tried not to notice, though her fingers itched to smooth wayward waves. Listening to his rich voice with the hint of accent did enough strange things to her insides. Looking at him was a killer.

"You sound like a travel brochure." She'd wanted to write those once upon a time, another career goal that hadn't worked out too well.

His gorgeous mouth tilted at the corners. "I could be. Montavia is—how do I express it?—an undiscovered treasure. A tiny alpine paradise. And I want to make the rest of the world aware of her great potential as a first-class resort area."

"Montavia?" Carly latched on to the word like a terrier on a T-bone. The name sounded familiar, but she couldn't bring up any data. "Exactly where is Montavia?"

Luc winced. He gathered the front of his hair and shoved it backward.

Dang. She'd wanted to do that.

As soon as the thought came, Carly thrust it out. She was onto something here. Getting distracted could get a P.I. killed. Well, maybe not here and now but somewhere. Besides, Luc had avoided revealing the name of his country. Why did it matter if she knew where he lived?

"Near Switzerland," he finally said and then, smooth as French silk pie, he glanced toward the food table and changed the subject. "Would you care for some of Carson's birthday cake?"

Yes, she'd have some cake, but she wanted some more answers, too. She jumped up from the table. To her everlasting dismay, one hand struck her half-empty tea glass. As if in slow motion, the glass tumbled forward and clattered onto the checkered cloth.

Carly squeezed her eyes shut. When she dared peek, sticky tea splattered the front of Luc's handsome shirt.

With a groan of dismay Carly grabbed her napkin and rushed to repair the damage. Now she'd done it. Luc would leave to change his clothes and never want to see her again.

Luc Gardner was secretive about his home, leery of the press and smelled deliciously rich. To a good detective those added up to one thing: he had to be *somebody*. And Carly, who desperately needed to prove she could investigate anybody, anywhere, and come up with something, needed to find out who.

Investigating him would keep her busy during this odious exile, and if Luc turned out to be nobody, no harm done. But if she was really, really lucky, Luc Gardner just might be the answer to her prayers.

If her clumsiness didn't kill him first.

Chapter Three

Regardless of one's location, sunrise was a shockingly vulgar time of day.

These were Carly's first thoughts as she crawled from beneath her star-of-Bethlehem quilt and stumbled across the polished oak floors into the bathroom. What had possessed her to agree to a trail ride at sunrise?

She'd forgotten to ask when breakfast was served and she'd bet a mocha Frappuccino there wasn't a Starbucks within a hundred miles.

In the city, where there was nothing but concrete and cars, morning arrived with the sounds of horns honking, sirens screaming and trucks roaring past. Good sounds. Normal stuff.

But out here in the Oklahoma outback, some love-struck bird had chosen her windowsill to belt out his twittering happiness. And above the air-conditioning she heard cows mooing. Any minute she expected a rooster to cut loose.

Might as well get used to it. Exile could last a long time.

She showered and dressed, hoping her Payless hiking boots would do for horseback riding. Not that she knew much about that dubious activity, but she was game. Sort of.

She tossed her camera over one shoulder and started out the door. Sunrise was a sight she didn't plan to see too often. Might as well get some shots.

Near the reception desk she looked for signs of life, planning to ask about breakfast—especially coffee—but the area was empty, lit only by small security lights. Disappointed, Carly headed toward the riding stables.

The air was fresh and filled with the fragrance of some sweet blossom she couldn't name, a decided improvement on exhaust fumes. An orange glow, like a distant fire, hovered on the eastern horizon.

Carly lifted her camera and waited for that perfect moment when the sun would streak the sky in dazzling colors.

"Lovely, isn't it?"

The masculine voice coming from behind in the semi-darkness startled her. She jerked around. Her camera went off, and Luc Gardner tossed an arm over his eyes.

"Oh, I am so sorry." Carly rushed to him as if she'd sprayed him with Mace. Which she might have done had she been carrying any.

"No," he said with that whisper of an accent. "It is I

who apologizes. I should have made my presence known."

"I'm sorry. Really. But it's a little creepy out here in the dark for a city girl."

He cocked his head, interested. Even in the twilight he was brilliantly handsome in his boots and jeans, and even though he wore a hat, she knew what was under it. "Have you always lived in a city?"

"Dallas suburbs mostly. Grandma lived out in the country, but I never spent the night there." She gave a fake shudder. "Coyotes."

"Then why choose a guest ranch for your vacation?"

Choose wasn't the correct word. Neither was *vacation*. "A little gift from my sister." An egg-yolk sun had broken over the horizon and was really showing off. "I can't believe you're still speaking to me after the tea incident last night."

Luc smiled and Carly's stomach went south. "Accidents happen."

He had that right. And if he was smart, he'd run backward instead of standing next to her. She turned to snap a picture of the radiant sky.

"Accidents not only occur, they follow me like homeless puppies." She peeked over one shoulder, hoping he wouldn't disappear but believing he had every reason to do so. "Are you headed out on the trail ride?"

"Yes. Are you?"

"Afraid so. Although I'm still wondering how Teddi talked me into it. I am not a morning person. Nor do I know much about riding horses."

She started walking. Luc fell in step beside her.

"Are you sure you want to walk next to me?" Carly asked. "The sky could fall, you know."

"Though I quake from the mere thought, I will be brave."

Carly chuckled, appreciating his humor and the way he downplayed the tea incident. Luc, the cowboy-god with bad-boy hair, was a pretty nice guy.

"Just keep your distance when we approach the horses. No doubt I'll be pummeled by an obstinate equine."

They rounded the house and neared the stable, where a dozen saddled horses and several wranglers were already waiting out in front. She made note of the fact that Cranky Carson—her name for the dour ranch owner—was not present. Good. Getting up this early was bad enough without looking at that sour puss.

"You'll do fine with these horses," Luc said. "They are all trained to follow the lead animal and are as docile as lambs. No pummeling allowed. And they know the trails better than the cowboys."

She certainly hoped so. Lifting her camera, she snapped. The horses didn't move, but one of the wranglers turned to look at her.

"Do you serve coffee on this wilderness trek?" she said with a caffeine-deprived snarl.

From beside her came a low chuckle. "The ride only lasts an hour. Espresso will be waiting when we return."

Carly groaned with gratitude. "Ah, the nectar of the gods."

She raised her camera to snap another picture. Curiously Luc moved aside, avoiding her aim.

"Camera shy?" she asked.

"I would not want to ruin your scenic photos."

As if he could.

One of the wranglers stepped forward and doffed his hat. "Morning, ma'am. Remember me? Dirk? We met last night at the cookout."

He was nice-looking in a cowboy kind of way, with pleasant hazel eyes and laugh crinkles, but the dip of snuff in his bottom lip was a real turnoff. "Morning, Dirk."

"There will be plenty of wildlife and such out on the trial for you to take pitchers of."

Carly refused to grin at his pronunciation of *pictures*.

"Thanks, Dirk. I'll keep my eye out."

"Mr. Gardner is great at spottin' about any critter in the woods. He'll point them out to you, won't you, Mr. Gardner."

"With great pleasure."

The wrangler headed back to his duties. Carly turned a curious gaze toward Luc. He was one of the few men taller than she, and the experience of tilting her head to meet his gaze was pretty cool.

"I thought you'd only been here two days."

He offered an elegant shrug, his white Western shirt stretching over broad shoulders. "I ride out often. Horses are a great passion of mine."

She'd bet he was passionate about a lot of other things, too. Passionate enough to master anything he chose. The thought gave her a startlingly sensual shudder. She, Carly the loveless, never entertained such notions. Must be the lack of caffeine.

A family of five from Ohio arrived at that moment. Or, in Carly's estimation, the parents arrived. The two young boys whooped and jumped, startling the horses, the birds and everything else within earshot. The teenage girl, in a skintight T-shirt that displayed her belly piercing, sulked.

"Why did we have to get up so early?" the girl asked. "I hate this vacation. It's so boring." Suddenly her gaze landed on Luc and a radical change occurred. She straightened from her slouch and smiled. "Good morning, Luc."

The petulance was gone, replaced by an out-and-out purr. For someone bored, she sounded downright perky. Carly rolled her eyes. Sheesh.

Luc responded with a polite greeting and then said to Carly, "I will let you know when we come upon a good area for photographs."

When he moved away to mount a waiting horse, the teen tossed her head and made a beeline for a wrangler holding the reins of a drowsy pony. She gave the cowboy the same fluttery eyelashes and made a pretense of needing way too much help onto the horse. Carly couldn't resist snapping a picture.

Hanging the camera around her neck, Carly approached her own mount with trepidation. Dirk offered a hand up. Once she'd swung into the saddle and the Appaloosa hadn't budged, she breathed a sigh of relief.

Dirk grinned up at her and gave the horse a pat. "You'll do all right, Miss Carly. Don't fret. Stormy is as easygoing as an old hound dog. And I'll be right here if you need help."

Poor cowboy had no idea that he was talking to Carly the Klutz. If old Stormy had a buck in him, she would find it. "Thanks, Dirk."

She squeezed the saddle horn so hard it should have honked. Dirk handed her the reins, and thankfully Stormy remained as docile as promised.

Luc's horse, on the other hand, hadn't stood still for a second. As the intriguing man swung a nicely muscled leg over the saddle, the large black animal whickered, tossed his proud head and pranced backward. Luc handled the animal with the expertise of someone who had ridden forever.

The rest of the guests mounted along with the wranglers, and they were off, single file down a well-worn path. One cowboy rode to each side, with the other in the lead. Carly noted right away that Luc did not follow the pack but rode where he pleased to talk to the other riders. Darn her eyes for following him. He was a fascinating man. After last night, her P.I. antennae quivered violently. That was the reason she watched him. Curiosity. Plain and simple.

Stuck between Dirk in the lead and the teenage girl, Carly hoped a conversation with the teen would take her mind off the stunning man aboard the magnificent black.

The saddle creaked as she twisted around and spoke to the girl behind her. "I'm Carly Carpenter."

"Tina Osborne," the teen answered.

Osborne. It figured. She, Carly the Klutz, would end up exiled with the namesake of Ozzy and his dysfunctional crew.

"Of *the* Osborne family?" she asked just for orneriness.

Tina gave her the annoyed look teenagers reserve for the ultrastupid. "I get asked that all the time."

"It must get tiring to be mistaken for such a famous family."

"Yeah." Tina sliced a look toward Luc, who galloped the beautiful black steed. "Isn't he dreamy?"

"If you like that type."

Or if you were a breathing female between the ages of one and a hundred.

"Omigosh, look. He's coming this way."

Carly's stomach did a weird leap. Considering she'd had no breakfast, she wasn't the least surprised.

Luc reined the black alongside.

Holding the smooth leather reins in a death grip, Carly pointed at Luc's spirited stallion. "Don't park that demon horse near me."

The corner of his mouth tilted. "Why not?"

"I'm afraid he'll give Stormy ideas, and he'll try to live up to his name."

Luc's teeth flashed. "Zeus will behave."

Sure enough, the black pranced, head high, but stayed right where Luc put him. Even a testosterone-driven stallion with enough pent-up energy to fuel a city fell prey to Luc Gardner's commanding charm. "Around that line of trees is a pond. You may want to have your camera ready."

"Do you think we'll see any wildlife?" she asked.

"Yesterday two does with their fawns and a great blue heron drank there. There are also red fox, raccoon and sometimes even bald eagles. We aren't far from the river, so any type of wild creature may be near."

Carly widened her eyes. "Coyotes?"

Luc chuckled, blue eyes dancing with mischief. "You never know."

She perched a fist on one hip. "Would you tell me if there were?"

With a laugh he reined the horse around and galloped off, a golden god aboard a stunning black horse. Carly was tempted to snap a picture but didn't want him getting ideas. Neither did she want to fall off her horse, a distinct possibility with her knees trembling this way.

Tina, whom Carly had momentarily forgotten, spoke in a hushed voice. "Are you two dating?"

Now it was Carly's turn to laugh. Imagine thinking someone like Luc would be interested in Carly the Klutz.

By midmorning Carly was back in her room, backside sore and belly growling. Coffee cup in hand, she dived for the remaining banana in her fruit basket and thought about the trail ride. Much more pleasant than she'd expected. They'd spotted several deer and a couple of turkeys. They had also disturbed a covey of quail.

And then there was Luc, with his easy smile and wild golden hair. She'd had to work much too hard not to salivate or stare at him too much. But she had to admit his presence had somehow energized the trail ride.

She perused the schedule for something to do, found

nothing of interest and wandered over to her laptop and flipped it on.

She found an e-mail from Lester the Molester, which she deleted without answering.

There was also a note from her sister, Meg, telling her to have a good time with some hot cowboy. Not even a hint that she was forgiven and could come back to work. She deleted that without answering, too. Her sister, who looked like a darker-haired Julia Roberts, found her lack of feminine wiles sad and confusing. Carly's parents likewise had seemed befuddled by their misfit daughter who never cared if she had a boyfriend, would rather watch the travel channel than have her hair done and didn't even try to compete with Marvelous Meg.

E-mail out of the way, she opened a new document. Even without a case to document she was a meticulous note keeper. Why not chronicle her day? After five minutes she stopped to reread. Every paragraph had Luc's name in it.

"Sheesh." She shook her head at the screen. "What is wrong with me?"

And then, like a sign from above, an idea came. She clicked on the Internet and typed Luc's name into the search engine.

Nothing came up. Weird. If he was *somebody,* he would be listed on the Internet.

For the heck of it she typed in Montavia, the name of his native country, and was inundated with hits. She clicked on one, read a bit about the history of a small kingdom in the Alps. Out of curiosity, she clicked on several other sites and found photos of lovely villages nestled in green valleys. Luc had not been exaggerating with his description.

Yet another site caught her eye. It was a newspaper article about the death of the crown prince of Montavia in a skiing accident several years ago. Gleaning the details, she read about the prince's family, the Jardines. King Alexandre and Queen Aurora and two siblings, Anastasia and Luc.

"Luc?" Her ears began to buzz with the kind of anticipation reserved only for when she was about to discover something important.

Fingers shaky with excitement, she searched through more photos until she found a formal portrait of the royal family of Montavia.

A smile the size of Texas Stadium nearly cracked her jaw. For there, standing tall and serious in a military uniform, was none other than her drugstore cowboy, Luc Gardner. It was him, all right. Even with his hair cropped short there was no mistaking that movie-star face.

Her curiosity went wild. Why would the heir to the throne of anywhere be here—alone? Why wasn't he surrounded by bodyguards and an entourage of servants?

She struck another key, scrolling and searching for more information. Somewhere, someone knew the answer.

Part of her job—most of her job, if she admitted the truth—was spent doing Internet and data searches. She'd become adept at ferreting out sources. Court records, police records, newspapers all proved invaluable to a detective.

Prince Luc—she got a little shiver at the way that sounded—had no criminal record, nor had he filed any complaints, but the European newspapers were on him like subway rats on a cheeseburger. Most of the articles were old, but the playboy prince, as they called him, had generated plenty of press.

Suddenly her breath quickened at a headline dated two days before: Playboy Prince Missing.

Missing? She batted her eyes at the screen. Luc was missing?

As she read the article, her fertile mind went wild. Luc had ditched his bodyguards and disappeared. No one knew where he had gone. The palace feared for his safety. Some royal advisor named Count Broussard was offering a reward for information concerning the whereabouts of the missing prince.

A thrill of victory rippled from Carly's brain to her fingertips.

Luc was missing. This count dude wanted to find him. And she just happened to be a private investigator who could do the job. Never mind that she already knew where Luc was. Count Broussard didn't need to know that. If she pretended to have a lead now and revealed the prince's whereabouts in a couple of days, she would make a little money, get her job back and earn her boss's respect.

Fingers shaking with excitement, she whipped out her calling card, grabbed for the telephone and asked for an overseas operator.

At last, at last, at last. Carly the Klutz was onto a case of her own, and there was nothing Eric or Meg could do to stop her.

Chapter Four

She'd done it.

With a whoop of joy Carly executed a perfectly acceptable pirouette in the center of her hardwood floor—acceptable for a ballerina in hiking boots, that is.

The die was cast. There was no turning back.

Melodramatic as a *Dragnet* episode, Carly flopped onto the bed and hugged herself.

Count Broussard, royal advisor to the crown prince of Montavia, had fallen for her little white lies. In fractured French she'd convinced him that she had a lead on Luc's whereabouts and could be on her way to his possible location in a matter of hours.

The count had been overjoyed. Carly's P.I. antennae had quivered just a bit at what amounted to the man's excess eagerness to give her the job, but she'd waved away the red flag. The poor man was worried about

Luc's well-being. Naturally he'd be anxious to find someone willing and able to locate the second most important man in his kingdom.

There was only one flaw in Carly's otherwise perfect plan. Forced to give Wright Stuff Investigations as a reference—and to hint in veiled terms that the agency was her own—Carly would have to ask Meg to cover for her. Somehow, without revealing everything, she'd find a way.

This case was too important and too exciting to allow such a tiny detail to interfere. In the end, Meg would thank her, Eric would give her a job and a raise and she would be forever and always a bona fide private investigator.

The next afternoon Carly leaned into the small bathroom mirror doing something she hadn't done since eighth grade—trying on makeup. She didn't know why. But then, life was a mystery. She didn't know why she did lots of things.

As she stroked her lashes with mascara, a gunshot broke the silence.

Carly jabbed herself in the eye.

The wand clattered into the sink. Black watery streaks slithered down the drain.

A second gunshot sounded. She rubbed streaming tears from one red eye and rushed to the window. No war planes on the horizon.

Either Cranky Carson had lost it and was eliminating the guests or a wild-game hunt was going on in the backyard.

Better check it out. She had a crown prince to protect. Okay, so she wasn't a bodyguard, but she could be. She still owned a stun gun.

Shoving her feet into brogans, Carly grabbed her camera and bounded down the stairs. More booms ripped the country quiet.

She followed the sound to an area far from the house. Keeping low, she darted from tree to tree. Just as she ran out of cover, a voice shouted, "Pull!" followed by another sonic boom.

Carly wilted against the smooth bark of a cotton-wood.

Darn. Skeet shooting. What a letdown.

But as soon as she spotted the shooter's wild, unruly golden hair, her disappointment winged off into the afternoon sunshine. An uncharacteristic quiver of pleasure shimmered down her arms.

Luc. The incognito prince.

As unobtrusively as possible she snapped a picture and then moseyed into the clearing. Hay bales formed a protective barrier about thirty yards square.

"Pull!" The clay pigeon soared upward and exploded in midair.

To make her presence known and minimize the risk of becoming a pigeon herself, Carly applauded. "Great shot."

Luc lowered the rifle and turned, expression bright. He reached up and looped a pair of ear covers around his neck.

"Hello. Have you come to try your luck?"

She shook her head. Her hair flopped loose and grazed her cheek. "Never fired a shotgun in my life."

A handgun, yes. Shotgun, no.

"Care to have a go at it?"

"Have you forgotten the tea incident or my propensity for damaging everything in my wake?"

Luc grinned. "I enjoy living dangerously."

A thrill jumped around in her belly. Exactly what she needed. More opportunity to spend time with the hideaway prince. More chances to snap photos that would prove to Count Broussard that she had indeed discovered Luc's whereabouts.

The idea of participating in any activity with Luc was downright titillating—in a professional manner of speaking, of course. Carly was immune to stunningly handsome, unerringly polite, genuinely nice crown princes.

Sort of.

"All right, then. What do I do?"

Other women might shy away from guns, but not Carly. She was nothing if not a gamer.

Admiration flashed in Luc's bluer-than-blue eyes. He felt in his vest pocket and came out with a set of earplugs. "You will need these. Hearing is still possible, but they will muffle the gunshot."

He waited while she poked the rubber plugs in each ear, then motioned to a spot slightly behind his right arm. "Stand back here. I will demonstrate."

Though itching to snap a picture, Carly did as she was told. Watching Luc do anything was worth the wait.

Luc elevated the rifle to shoulder level, aligning his cheek with the butt of the gun. His stance was erect and sure, his hands steady and relaxed. The slight breeze ruffled his curls.

"Observe my body position carefully."

Yeah, right. As if she wasn't already.

For a man so tall, he moved with easy grace, his beautifully proportioned body broad at the shoulders, lean as a lion everywhere else. Athletic muscles rippled beneath his crisply ironed gray shirt. Carly thought a prince should be more delicate, softer, but Luc looked strong enough to handle anything. Royal or not, he was all man.

She swallowed to moisten a throat gone annoyingly dry. Think business, Carly. Business.

Luc continued the muffled instructions, but Carly didn't comprehend a word.

When the gunshot exploded, she jumped, bobbling her camera.

Luc lowered the rifle and turned. "Were my instructions clear enough?"

"Oh, yes. Very clear." It was my head that was messed up, not the instructions.

"Ready to try your hand?" He extended the shotgun.

She shrugged, pretending a confidence she did not feel. Shooting a Glock at the firing range was one thing. Shooting a shotgun with a too-gorgeous-to-live crown prince nearby was quite another. "Sure."

He whipped off his vest. "Wear this." At her lifted eyebrow, he explained, "To protect your shoulder."

She poked her arms into the garment and suffered a self-conscious moment when Luc stepped in front to raise the zipper. The mild heat and subtle scent of his body wrapped around her like an embrace. He was so close, so considerate—and so big that Carly felt positively fragile and utterly feminine.

As if that was possible.

Shrugging off the silly notion, she lifted the surprisingly heavy firearm and tried to imitate Luc's stance.

"Relax your shoulders." Voice low and patient, Luc's accent whispered along her nerve endings. "No. That is not quite right. Allow me."

He stepped behind her and aligned his body with hers. His front pressed to her back. His arms stretched over hers. His hand folded around her fingers.

Okay. Now she was having flights of fantasy totally improper for a professional. The man was a crown prince, for heaven's sake.

"You and the weapon must become as one." He jiggled her shoulder with his and murmured against the sensitive flesh behind her ear, "Relax."

Carly drew in a steadying breath, determined to concentrate on the sport instead of the strong, elegant hands and broad, muscular body touching her in more places than she'd been touched in a long time. It was much harder than she imagined.

"Excellent. Widen your eyes just before the shot and remember to control your breathing."

As if she could. Right now her breath was jammed somewhere in the vicinity of her toenails.

"Okay," she said. "Let's do it." Rats. That didn't come out right. "The shooting thing, I mean."

Luc's chuckle vibrated through her body. "As surely

we shall," he replied. "When ready, call 'Pull,' and the two of us together will move only our front arms, following the target until right before it reaches its apex. Then gently slap the trigger, taking care not to jerk the gun off aim."

She knew that part. But somehow the idea of moving any part of her body with Luc's didn't have a thing to do with shooting clay pigeons.

"Here we go." With a deep breath and shoulders as relaxed as possible, she shouted the signal, listened for the *clack* of the releasing skeet and followed the ascent with more concentration than she'd thought possible.

Luc's body moved with hers, guiding, coaxing, until that perfect moment when she pulled the trigger.

Clay pieces shattered and tumbled from the sky like fat confetti.

"Excellent." Luc stepped away, face alight. "You have a sharp eye and a smooth trigger finger. I am impressed."

"You are?" Her heart raced, and she didn't even want to analyze the reasons.

He took the shotgun for reload.

"Shall we do it again?"

"You are a very brave man, Mr. Gardner."

His lips twitched with amusement. "I was standing behind you. No danger lurks in back of the gun."

Carly cocked her head, pretending insult. "For that crack, you have to take my picture. My sister will love it."

She bent to retrieve her camera from the grass and traded it to Luc for the reloaded firearm.

"Your sister is the one who arranged this vacation, no?"

As if Carly needed the reminder. "Yes. Marvelous Meg."

She shouldered the weapon.

"You are close with your sister Meg?"

"Very close. How about you? Any sibs?" She knew the answer but figured what the heck. Let the man use that accent.

"Sibs?" He frowned only a second before his quick mind interpreted the shortened term. "Ah, siblings. Yes. A sister. Anna."

Only her name is Anastasia, not Anna. "Is she as gorgeous as…?" You? She bit the inside of her lip in time to change directions. "Is she beautiful?"

"Most people say so. I find her to be a pest most of the time." Affection gleamed on his face. "And what of your sister? Is Meg as lovely as you?"

Carly lowered the shotgun and turned to look at him. "I'm afraid you've lost me there. But yes, Meg is gorgeous. Too beautiful for words and anything but a pest. If she wasn't such a great person, I'd hate her."

"And why is that?"

The subject was far too complicated to go into, so Carly said, "Are you going to take my picture shooting this poor little clay thingie or not?"

Eyes merry, he raised the camera and took aim. "Indeed I am."

"You shoot me. I'll shoot the pigeon." Shotgun to her shoulder, Carly took aim, gave the signal, fired…and missed by a mile.

"Aw, shucks. No clay pigeons for supper tonight. My ten young'uns will go hungry again."

Luc chuckled. "Try another. We cannot allow starving children."

At that moment Teddi Benedict came flitting through the line of trees from the vicinity of the main house.

"Yoo-hoo. Hel-lo. I thought I heard shooting."

With exuberant cheer she waved both hands, her greeting taking in Luc, Carly and the ranch hand in the background working the shooting range. A half dozen colorful bracelets rattled up and down her slender arms.

"Would you care to join us?" Luc asked with his usual courtesy. "I'm giving lessons today."

"And he's a great teacher," Carly said. "Better take him up on it."

Bright orange earrings the size and shape of pancakes danced as Teddi shook her head. "No, thank you. I loathe guns. They interfere with the balance of my yin and yang. Something about the improper dispersal of cosmic energy."

"Ah," said Luc.

"Well," said Carly, searching for some sensible reply until she realized there was none. "We were just taking some vacation photos to send to our sisters."

"Really?" Teddi's hazel eyes lit up. "You both have sisters? That is so cool. Any ornery brothers like mine?"

"None for me," Carly said.

"What about you, Luc?"

Luc's expression tightened. Pain flashed but disappeared quickly behind his perfect poise. Carly ached for him. "I lost my only brother in an accident a few years ago."

Teddi's elfin face twisted with compassion. "Oh, sweetie, I'm so sorry. Please forgive me." With a quick-silver shift she said, "Let me have the camera and I'll take a picture to send to your sister. She'll love this. Get over there by Carly and ham it up." She shoved Luc in Carly's direction, her small hands fluttering. "Y'all are just so cute by each other. Both of you are tall. And she's so dark and you're so blond. That opposite thing creates wonderful metaphysical karma, you know."

Carly could feel Luc's reluctance, but his innate manners would not let him refuse. She should have felt badly for his dilemma, but instead she was pleased. The more photos, the better. So what if she liked standing close to Luc, looking into those oceanic eyes and seeing that glorious smile. She wasn't crazy enough to think this teeny-tiny attraction could ever amount to anything. But nothing in her detective manual said she couldn't enjoy it.

Luc cleared his throat and allowed Teddi to pose him beside the interesting Carly. To avoid having his picture taken, he would have to make a scene. Doing so would raise suspicions, and this was only one woman's vacation photo, not something that would emblazon the cover of a tabloid. No one would discover from this simple snapshot that he was on the Benedict Ranch.

"Oh, wait," Teddi said, pointing to the rifle. "Y'all hold that gun up like real shooters. Luc, stand behind Carly and show her how." She fluttered her hands. "You know. Make it look real."

Luc and Carly exchanged glances. Had Teddi been

watching earlier when he had demonstrated the proper shooting form?

"That's not necessary," Carly said a little too quickly, her clear skin flushing a rather pretty shade of rose. "Just snap the pictures."

"That's no fun. Come on, Luc. Pose pretty for the camera."

For reasons he chose not to explore, Luc wanted another opportunity to be up close and personal with the beguiling Miss Carpenter. Surely her skin was not as soft nor her scent as gently flowered as he thought.

"I fear," he said to Carly, "that she will not desist until we do her bidding."

"I just love the way he talks sometimes, don't you, Carly? Now be nice and do my bidding."

Teddi's pixie grin and exuberance would charm the skin off a snake. Luc could not resist a laugh as he hefted the shotgun and placed it in Carly's hands.

"Pose for the lady. Then perhaps she will go away."

Teddi found that wildly funny. "I will, I will. I promise."

Luc stepped behind Carly and assumed his previous instructor's position. He'd done this many times with youngsters who wanted to learn the sport, but never before had the action seemed so personal. Carly's skin was indeed every bit as soft and her scent deliciously clean and floral.

When he leaned against her back and slid his arm alongside hers, a tiny quiver ran through her. The reaction surprised—and pleased—him.

Only by calling upon discipline learned from birth

could he resist nuzzling the soft skin behind her ear. Foolish, ridiculous notion.

Yet his mind had been distracted from the moment he'd first touched her. And when she'd bent to retrieve the camera and her loose skirt had edged upward, his body had reacted in a most inappropriate manner. She had long, glorious legs, far too lovely to be covered by an ugly brown skirt.

How could a woman who dressed so badly ooze femininity without even trying? Even Carly's delightfully disarrayed hair and the smudge of black beneath one red eye charmed him today. He wondered what had come over him. Was he so accustomed to having a woman on his arm at all times that he'd forgotten how to be alone?

Click.

"One more and I'm done," Teddi said, merrily breaking into his confused thoughts.

Click.

"There you go." Teddi returned the camera to Carly, who quickly stepped away. And just as quickly Luc wished her back.

"All this shooting has misaligned my chi, so if y'all will excuse me, I need to consult my crystals before lunch." A frown puckered between Teddi's light brown eyebrows. "Or is that my tea leaves? I get those two mixed up sometimes. Oh, well. I'm off. You two have fun and I'll catch up to you at dinner."

Colorful and flighty as a monarch, Teddi flitted away, across the open field and into the trees. Luc had the fanciful notion that she might be a wood nymph.

"She seems so normal most of the time."

Carly shoved a lock of loose hair behind one ear. Luc stifled the urge to pull the entire pile free from its topknot.

"Pardon if I disagree. Though Carson's sister is a delight, she never does anything remotely normal. Did you know she believes herself to be the reincarnation of Queen Latifah?"

"But Queen Latifah isn't dead."

"Precisely."

Their eyes locked and both burst out laughing. To his relief, the uncomfortable attraction that had simmered in the air dissipated. Carly was a bright woman, charming in a waiflike manner and totally unlike any female he'd ever known. She would provide occasional distraction from his worries, but he need not worry about becoming involved or having his name linked with hers in the tabloids. She was not his type any more than she was the kind of woman a royal was expected to wed. No fear of entanglements here. Being with Carly Carpenter on the Benedict Ranch was the safest place he could be.

Chapter Five

Carson Benedict tossed his trail-dusty hat on the desk and eased into the brown leather chair his grandmother had purchased as a gift on his twenty-first birthday. That was the day she'd also turned control of the ranch over to him. And in the years since, he'd worked his tail off only to find the ranch now slowly slipping out of his grasp. Teddi was right about one thing. With cattle prices down, he had to find a way to keep the guest rooms filled all the time.

Swiveling to his computer, he pulled up the bookings for the next month. Slim pickin's.

"Might as well face it, Carson." Teddi came flitting through his office door. "I consulted my energy map, and what we lack here is the harmonious conjunction of love and work. Changing the name to Love County

Love Ranch for singles would be a step toward realigning our yin and yang."

He swiveled away from the computer with a frown. Other than the crack about changing the name of his ranch, he didn't have a clue what she was talking about. He wasn't sure she did either. "You promised to drop that subject."

"I will. As soon as you win the bet."

Wretched bet. Why had he made it? "I'm working on it."

"I haven't seen you do one thing to encourage Luc and Carly. They won't be here forever, you know."

That stopped him in his tracks.

"Carly?" A suave, sophisticated prince and a bumbling blue-collar bag lady? "What about the new guest, Pammie Wilson? Wouldn't she be better suited to Luc?"

Teddi made one of those female faces that said he was so dense. "Not Pammie."

"She's pretty." Carson was having a hard enough time with the idea of playing matchmaker for his unsuspecting friend. He sure didn't want to push the wrong woman on him.

"Trust me on this, Carson. Not Pammie. Her center lacks spiritual unity." She took the paperweight from his desk and stared into it as if it were a crystal ball. "Besides, we bet that you couldn't match up the first two single guests. And Luc and Carly were the first. Haven't you seen the two of them talking? There's something there to build on already. I gave them both a mandarin duck."

"Excuse me?"

"You know. Feng shui. The mandarin duck is the symbol of love and romance."

"Ah." Feng shui or not, he *had* noticed Luc's solicitous manner with Carly at dinner last night. And later they'd been laughing over something that had happened on the trail ride. He'd also observed the way Carly's eyes followed Luc's every move.

But why wouldn't Carly be enamored? Luc was suave and good-looking and always showed women the greatest courtesy. They fell for him like bricks from a ten-story building. It didn't have a thing to do with ducks or fungus.

"So will you do it? Will you give a little push to a budding romance? Or should I load those romance ads onto the Web site for you?"

Carson rubbed the back of his neck. "Seems like an underhanded thing to do to a man."

"Not if he likes her," Teddi said with uncanny wisdom. "*And* if you want me to shut up about the Love County Love Ranch."

Well. There was that.

Carly was late.

Dinner, a family-style affair in the enormous Benedict dining room, had begun five minutes ago. She hated being late. Everyone always stared at her. But she'd spent half an hour e-mailing info to the count and then for some weird reason she'd wanted to shower and wash her hair before coming down.

And now she had to pay the price.

Forks clattered and china clanked and the hum of

voices drifted out into the hall along with the smell of hot biscuits. Her stomach growled in appreciation.

Smoothing her hands down the sides of her skirt, she entered the room. Though conversation did not stop, a sea of faces turned to watch. And all her self-conscious tendencies leaped to the fore.

One of the faces looking her way was Luc's. Her insides somersaulted, but she blamed the roast turkey sitting smack in the middle of the long table. She'd always had a thing for juicy turkey browned to perfection.

Rounding the table, she headed toward the one empty place setting—the one between Tina Osborne and the prince himself. From the corner of one eye she glimpsed a cactus plant. What she didn't notice was the small, protruding branch. Her skirt caught on the spines, and the cactus teetered precariously, ready to fall if anyone so much as breathed hard.

She slammed on the brakes and tried to backtrack. Her skirt was parallel to the floor. A free shot of her thighs was there for the whole world to see, but she was afraid to move. The uncharitable cactus rocked from side to side. One wrong move and the pot would spill and the cactus would fill her legs with stickers.

In that split second when Carly realized she would once again humiliate herself, a masculine hand shot out and righted the tilted pot.

"Close one," Luc said, smiling into her eyes in a way that caused her stomach to do the somersault thing again.

Carly breathed a sigh of relief. "Thanks. I owe you."

Luc inclined his head, but she didn't miss the amusement in his eyes. A prickly feeling, as sharp as cactus, shot into her spine. So he thought she was a bumbling idiot. So he thought she was funny. Carly the Klutz, without an ounce of grace, an object of ridicule. Fine. She was used to it. She'd lived with this curse all her life, hadn't she?

Then why did it hurt more this time?

Luc held her chair, but she refused to meet his gaze. One stab in the pride was enough for one evening. If he laughed at her again, she might cry. Now how uncharacteristic was that?

"Thank you," she said stiffly. "I apologize for arriving late."

Carson Benedict scowled, but Teddi said, "You're on vacation. Think nothing of it." She passed Carly a bowl of creamed green peas.

Carly hated peas. But she'd already made enough of a scene, so she placed a spoonful on her plate.

Sometime during the day a couple of new guests had arrived. A blue-blooded mother and daughter from Maryland, both of them petite, blond and pretty. Carly felt like a Holstein cow.

The daughter, whose name was Pammie, had already lasered in on Luc and was regaling him with stories of her success in English riding circles. Pammie, it seemed, had been an alternate at the Olympic trials. An equestrian champion, she owned a prize jumper named Trident Spirit.

Luc listened and responded with interest, interjecting intelligent comments about the sport. Several times he looked to the other guests, trying to draw them into the conversation. But Carly had nothing intelligent to add. What exactly did one say about a horse named for sugarless chewing gum?

For the millionth time in her life she wished for fascinating hobbies to discuss. But who wanted to hear about the time she'd lain in a Dumpster all night to catch a cheating husband? And it was a rare person whose eyes didn't glaze over when she wanted to discuss something she'd watched on the travel channel.

When Carson Benedict aimed his black scowl her direction, she nearly choked on a biscuit.

"Have you been up to Sky Bluff yet, Miss Carpenter?"

Shaking her head, she gulped past the lump of bread and squeaked, "No. Never even heard of it."

"It's a must-see," the ranch owner continued. "Right, Luc?"

Luc turned from the blond Pammie to smile at Carly. She refused to acknowledge the tiny leap of pleasure. "Absolutely. You can see for miles. It's especially beautiful at sunset."

"Why don't you take Carly up there sometime? She might want some pictures."

Would the shock never end? For a taciturn fella, Carson was chatty tonight.

"It would be my distinct pleasure. We can either ride up or take the Jeep. Which would you prefer?"

Her mind screamed for the Jeep, but after listening to Pammie simper about her equestrian expertise and knowing Luc loved to ride, Carly said, "The horses would be great."

"Excellent choice. We can enjoy the scenery much better from horseback. There's a bald eagle nest along the ridge."

Pammie emitted a high-pitched squeal. "Eagles. How divine. I've always wanted to see a bald eagle in the wild."

Luc expanded his invitation to include everyone at the table. Pammie accepted with great delight, shooting a triumphant smile toward Carly.

Yeah, right. As if Carly the Klutz was some kind of competition. As if Luc even knew she was alive. As if she had a chance of impressing a crown prince.

Luc's offer to escort her was a favor to Carson. Plain and simple. The man was a born diplomat. He even had the knack to make someone like her feel important. Diplomacy. Courtesy. Those were the only reasons he paid any attention to her at all.

It was clear he preferred pretty Pammie. What man wouldn't? And she was far more his type.

As long as Carly could go along and snap photos to use in her investigation, she would be happy.

Happy, happy, happy. Even if it killed her.

Carly lay on her dude ranch bed, bare feet propped on the headboard, telephone cradled against her ear. A Granny Smith apple perched on her belly along with a notepad and pencil.

The phone on the other end rang three times, during which Carly prayed that Meg, and not Eric, would answer.

She'd just gotten off the line with Luc's royal

advisor and needed to cover her tracks. The investigation into the missing prince was moving along more
rapidly than she'd planned. But that was a good thing.

After last night, when she'd felt a teeny twinge—
okay, it was a giant jab—of jealousy at Luc's attentions
to the pert and pretty Pammie, Carly wanted to get this
show on the road and over with.

"Wright Stuff Investigations."

Thank goodness. It was Meg.

She blew out a breath of relief. "Hi, sis."

"Carly! I'm glad you called. How is everything on
your little vacation?"

Carly made a face and traced the horseshoe-shaped
groove in the headboard with her big toe. Meg could
sugarcoat a weekend in a knife factory with Jack the
Ripper.

"Great."

"Met any hot cowboys yet?" Her sister would never
stop hoping. Poor thing.

"Nada."

"Oh, come on, Carly. There are men galore on that
ranch. I checked before sending…" Meg stopped short
of admitting what Carly already knew. She'd chosen
this place because the men outnumbered the woman.

"I don't want to talk about my love life, Meg. How's
Eric? Any progress on that front?"

A brief silence. "I'm still working on him."

Which meant even sex wasn't enough this time.

"Well, don't worry about it." She rubbed the apple
back and forth on the bedspread. "I have a little something going here, so I'm not ready to come home yet."

"What kind of something?" Was that a glimmer of suspicion she heard in Meg's voice?

Carly wished she could confide in her sister. And she would have except for Eric. Meg might understand. Eric would be unconvinced that Carly could pull off an investigation of this importance.

And it *was* important.

Luc's royal advisor had been ecstatic with the photos she'd e-mailed and had instructed her to keep up the good work. But Eric was a by-the-book kind of a guy. He would fire her on the spot.

"I'd rather not talk about it right now, but I do need a favor."

"Uh-oh." Carly could imagine the furrows between Meg's perfectly waxed eyebrows.

"Stop frowning. It'll give you wrinkles." She held the apple above her face for inspection. A few more rubs and she could see her reflection. "I'm only asking you to give me a great reference should anyone call to check my credentials."

"Someone already has. A guy with a funky accent."

Carly's heart stopped. She slowly lowered the apple to her chest.

The count hadn't mentioned that part, but then, she hadn't asked. She'd been too intent on jotting down his specific instructions: to stay on the case, to send further photos by e-mail ASAP and to prepare a dossier of Luc's activities. She'd thought this last a little odd, but then Count Broussard had explained that the palace had no wish to disturb the prince's sabbatical. They simply wanted to be certain he was safe and indulging only in activities that wouldn't endanger him. He was, after all, heir to the throne.

She could understand that. And when the count offered to increase her fee, Carly was positive she was doing everyone a great service. The Montavian court could relax. Luc would be protected by her constant vigilance and could go right on with his vacation. And she would prove once and for all that she was a detective to be reckoned with.

But Broussard wasn't a fool. He *had* checked up on her.

Trying to keep the anxiety out of her voice, she asked, "What did you tell him?"

"The truth. That you're smart and capable."

Sisterly love welled inside Carly. She swallowed a lump. "I love you."

"Why? Who is this guy? What's going on?"

"Meg, for once will you just trust me here? Don't say anything to Eric, and if you get any more phone calls from the guy with the foreign accent, go along with everything he says and then refer him to me."

"I don't like the sound of this."

"It's nothing bad, I promise."

"Tell me. Or I won't cover your behind."

Carly racked her brain but knew there was only one way to throw her sister off the scent. "Okay, I didn't want to admit this yet, but you're forcing my hand. I've met someone."

That much was true. She had met Luc. And just because he was way out of her league did not make her statement a lie.

A sisterly hiss of inhaled breath was followed by a long, low, "Eeeeee. I knew that place was going to be special."

Carly rolled her eyes toward the ceiling. *Special* was the right word.

"Before I get too involved, I want to make sure he's the real deal."

"Makes sense, especially after that drug dealer you dated." As if Carly needed the reminder. "Caution is always good. Is this guy from another country?"

"France." Not much of a stretch.

"Ooh la la. I've heard about those French lovers."

"Shut up, Meg," she said mildly.

Her sister's laughter trilled through the line. "Okay, but promise you will tell me everything—I mean absolutely every juicy detail—if this guy turns out to be a real hottie."

"You have my word. If he's everything I think he is, you will hear all about him when I come home."

Another truth.

"I need to hang up now, Meg. Someone is at my door."

"Maybe it's your French lover."

"Meg," she warned.

"'Bye, Carly. Remember, every juicy detail."

With a snort Carly disconnected and shoved off the bed, knocking her notepad and pencil to the floor.

"Who is it?" She tripped over her boots—the darned oversize things—and wondered why she didn't buy some decent shoes. She'd never noticed how ugly they were.

Pondering that little revelation, she kicked the hikers to one side and crunched into the apple on her way to the door.

Her visitor was almost as shocking as the sour apple juice. Carson Benedict stood there, hat in hand, looking decidedly uncomfortable. The creepy dog sat at his heel, staring at Carly with one blue eye.

She gulped down a mostly unchewed bite of apple. "Mr. Benedict."

"Miss Carpenter." His dark gaze flickered over her shoulder, down to the floor and then back to her face. He twisted his hat in a slow circle. "Don't know if you noticed on the schedule, but the boys are taking the chuck wagon out on a camping trip this afternoon. A cattle roundup. Thought you might want to go along."

"Camping? As in sleeping on the ground in the woods?"

"The ranch provides sleeping bags."

As if that made spending the night with coyotes a safe and acceptable activity.

"I thought everyone was going up to Sky Bluff this afternoon."

His glower deepened. "You don't want to go up there. All those women poking around. They'll scare the eagles away."

Hadn't the Sky Bluff outing been Carson's idea to begin with? And now he was warning her off.

"What about the other guests? Are they still going to Sky Bluff?"

"Another day. The roundup slipped my mind last night. Luc is going camping. You need to go, too."

She *needed* to go? What did he mean by that?

Carly stared at the lean, rangy rancher. Was the man as off-kilter as his sister? Nothing he said made sense.

But rational or not, Carson had just given her an excuse to spend more time investigating Prince Charming. Never mind that she didn't like the woods or the dark or the idea of sleeping without AC. If Luc was going off in the wilds to chase cows for two days, she had no choice but to do the same. Her career depended upon this case. And the royal court of Montavia expected her to keep Luc safe.

If the coyotes didn't get her first.

Chapter Six

Astride Zeus, Luc watched as the caravan of horses, wranglers, guests and the supply-laden chuck wagon pulled out of the gate shortly after lunch. The summer sun, relieved only by a fickle wind, glared white. In the distant west a couple of thunderheads made promises they probably wouldn't keep.

According to Dirk, the lead wrangler, they'd make camp before dark somewhere on the back side of the ranch, near Big Creek. Along the way guests would experience the thrill of rounding up whatever cattle they encountered in preparation for a move to another pasture.

Satisfaction filled his chest as he relaxed in the saddle and inhaled the rich scents of early summer. Sage and oak, the horses and leather, the nodding sunflowers and paintbrush. Everything smelled of peace.

He'd needed this rest, without the constant re-
minders from Arturo Broussard that he was not Philippe. He'd needed to be on his own, away from the
pressures, to think things through. Though no closer to
a decision now than before, he had at least found respite
here on Carson's ranch.

Except for his constant and altogether inappropriate
thoughts of a tall brunette with stunning legs.

He grinned in her direction. Sitting stiffly aboard the
plodding Stormy, Carly wrinkled her nose in response.
His grin widened.

The compelling Miss Carpenter. What was it about
her that drew his attention? He hadn't come here to be
distracted by women.

Pammie Wilson waved to him. He returned the greeting with a tip of his hat. She was the type of woman who
should have been a distraction, especially for a man in
his position. She would fit into his world. Yet he was not
drawn to her, did not find himself seeking her out.

Whereas Carly was…well, how did he say it? Carly
was natural. No pretense, no fluttery eyelashes or sly
looks. And she made him laugh. With her endearing
habit of bumbling into things and her wry humor, every
minute with her entertained.

She was dressed differently today. Gone was the
usual baggy outfit in favor of fitted jeans and a long-
sleeved man's shirt hanging open over a sunny yellow
tank top. He suffered a moment of regret that he hadn't
seen her mount the horse wearing those jeans. Her legs,
he already knew, were firm and shapely. Her backside
doubtless would be the same.

With a gentle nudge of his knees Luc turned Zeus and moved down the line until he reached Carly's side.

Feathery bits of hair, as richly colored as French coffee, had come loose and blew around her face.

"Where is your hat?"

Carly looped a lock of hair behind one ear. "Don't have one."

He slid a pointed glance toward the sun. "Why not? I thought the ranch supplied all necessary equipment."

"They do, but I refused. I don't burn easily." She pulled sunglasses from her pocket, tilted them toward him. "And I have my shades." With a grin she shoved them onto her face. "See? All fixed up."

The tiny frames barely covered her dark almond-shaped eyes. And supplied no protection from an afternoon in the direct sun. "Could I offer you my hat?"

"You could, but I wouldn't take it."

He'd suspected as much. "Let me know if you change your mind."

He knew she wouldn't do that either. Carly was a strong woman, not inclined to lean or cling.

"The sun doesn't bother me. I can ski all day without so much as a burn."

"You ski?" A cord of tension tightened in his chest. Skiing. His favorite—and most hated—sport.

"As a matter of fact, I do. Both kinds." Through the dark lenses she looked him over. "Let me guess. You snow ski. Like a champion, of course. Probably a few downhill cups on the trophy shelves."

"Why do you say that?" He hadn't skied in a very long time. Would never ski again.

She gave him a funny look. "Mountains, silly. Your country has mountains."

"Oh, of course. The mountains."

Unease made him shift on the saddle. Zeus tossed his head, jangled the reins. Luc was dismayed that she remembered his slip about Montavia but more dismayed at the gush of memories coursing through his head.

"Believe it or not," Carly went on, unmindful of his turmoil, "I can actually ski without killing myself or anybody else. Ever seen a one-footed water-skier?"

Water-skiing. He could think about that.

"Don't tell me."

"Yep. I can." She elevated one stirrup and wagged her boot. "With feet this size I could ski without skis."

Luc smiled.

"I can do flips, too."

"That I would like to see." And he meant it. His insides stirred at the idea of Carly in a bathing suit, long legs naked, performing acrobatics.

"Can you water-ski?"

"I would enjoy learning, but no, snow skis were my forte."

"*Were* your forte?"

Yes, his. But not his brother's, a topic he did not wish to discuss.

At the side of the trail a fat lizard caught his eye. Eager for a change in topics, he pointed it out. "What is that?" Covered in spiky scales, the grayish creature sunned himself on a rock. "A miniature triceratops?"

Carly chuckled. "It's a horned toad. But look out.

Some people say it spits blood, and if it hits your eye, you'll go blind."

In one quick motion Luc yanked his sunglasses from his pocket and shoved them into place. "Am I safe now?"

Her mouth, wide and full-lipped, quivered with a grin. His stomach responded in kind. She had an incredibly sexy mouth.

"Completely," she said, oblivious to his wayward thoughts. "When I was a kid, my parents wouldn't let us have a dog. One day I found a horny toad—that's what we called them—in Mom's flower bed. I named him Albert Einstein because he was so intelligent. I trained him to play dead whenever Mom came in the room—" She stopped. A blush bloomed on her cheekbones. "Sorry. That was boring."

"On the contrary." He suppressed a grin. "A… horny…toad named Albert Einstein is fascinating."

And so was she. For a moment he had a vision of her as a child, her knees dirty and skinned, her eyes as big as her entire face. She had dark, lovely eyes. So lovely that he resented the narrow strip of sunglasses that hid them.

"My family had many pets—a menagerie, one might say. My brother once owned a parrot who could squawk every note of Beethoven's Fifth."

Carly's laughter rang out over the wide-open space. "You only said that to make me laugh."

"No. I promise. Every word is true." But he enjoyed her laughter. "Philippe spent hours training that bird."

A grasshopper whirred onto her shirt, but she ignored it, her gaze intent on Luc instead. When she spoke, her tone was quiet, gentle.

"You miss him a lot, don't you?"

He glanced away from her compassionate face. The familiar ache that was his brother's memory started up again.

"Terribly. Every minute." He watched a pair of iridescent dragonflies lilt across the open sky, their gossamer beauty a reminder of how fragile life was.

"Tell me about him."

He brought his gaze back to her, found her watching him closely, her dark brown eyes gentle behind her shades.

"It's difficult. My family doesn't like to speak of him." Ah, but he wanted to. Needed to so badly at times.

"What a shame," she said mildly.

And he saw that it was, but he'd been taught to hold the suffering inside, as was befitting a royal. Even during that awful time when the press had made veiled accusations and gossip had run amok, the palace had kept quiet. Mother and Father had mourned in private seclusion. Only Anastasia, as he recalled, had howled and screamed like a mad thing. He'd envied her that release.

"When my sister and I were kids, we did lots of crazy things. Tell me the funniest thing you and Philippe ever did."

Carly wasn't going to let it go. And for once he didn't mind. Carly, with her unpretentious kindness, had no hidden agenda. He could talk to her.

Memories of his brother and him tumbled over each other. The funniest thing that ever happened to them was on the ski slopes. But it hurt too much to talk about that day.

"We were eleven and twelve, as I recall. One of the court—" He caught his error, glanced sideways. Carly remained unperturbed, so he went on. "One of my father's employees was not fond of children. Naturally he was the object of our most mischievous adventures."

"Naturally." She folded her hands on the saddle horn and leaned forward, face eager. "So tell me. What havoc did you wreak upon this poor guy?"

A breeze tossed a lock of hair across her mouth. Luc stifled the urge to smooth it back.

"This employee was our tutor of sorts, the man charged with our refinement." He paused to grin. "Not an easy task, I assure you, to convince two boys that a trip to the opera or the museum was as important as riding our ponies."

"Were you bad boys then?" She seemed delighted at the prospect.

"Not Philippe. My brother was the quiet one. The good son. I, on the other hand…" He raised and lowered one shoulder.

Carly's giggle tickled Luc's nerve endings like sweet music. "Bad-boy Luc. Yep. I can see it."

He'd been called that more times than he could count. "Our tutor was very controlling. Particularly of Philippe."

He, on the other hand, had been mostly ignored by Arturo unless he had caused some commotion. Which was more often than not.

"If your brother was the good boy, why was he harder on him?"

How did he explain to her that the life and education of a crown prince is very different from the norm?

"Because he was the heir. The tutor's job was to school him well, train him properly, see that he was cultured. In these things Artie did an excellent job. But he expected perfection in all areas."

"And you excelled, so he focused on Philippe."

"Not quite." Luc, the second son, was the troublesome afterthought, the stubborn one. Artie had not been able to browbeat him as he had Philippe. "My brother was far more adept at his lessons than I. He was quiet, studious, ever anxious to please, but he also tended to gain weight easily. Our tutor found his chubbiness unbecoming for a boy of his position and even controlled his diet."

The press, in its infinite cruelty, had once referred to Philippe as "the pudgy prince." Arturo had saved the article, using it as ammunition in his war against snacks.

"And you didn't like that much, did you?"

"How do you know?"

"The fierce expression on your face tells all."

"We hated it. And so, as we often did, we plotted our revenge. Or rather, I plotted. Philippe worried." But his brother had always gone along in the end after a bit of cajolery and, to Luc's way of thinking, had been the better for it. Most of the time.

Carly brightened and sat up straight. "You were the rebel. The ornery one."

"Let's just say I did not always follow directions well." Arturo had referred to him as a spawn of Satan more than once. Much to his delight. "One day a giant box of hand-dipped gourmet truffles arrived for our tutor, a gift from a highly important client."

"What did you do?" She squinted at him, eyes dancing. "Sneak in and eat the entire box?"

"Of course." He could still picture Philippe, chocolate smeared around his smiling mouth. That had been a particularly satisfying prank. "But we did more than that."

"Hot dang. My kind of guys."

"We had stables, remember. Each of us had a special pony. So we substituted very small horse—" How did one say *manure* delicately?

"Road apples," Carly finished for him, her lush mouth widening in a smile. "We call them road apples." She giggled. "Don't tell me he ate one."

A tiny smile tickled the corners of his mouth. "We can only hope."

She had laughed before about the singing parrot, but this time she howled. And Luc joined her.

How long had it been since he'd remembered Philippe with anything but pain. Interesting how the tragedy of death sometimes overshadows the happiness. But Carly had forced him to remember the joy.

Carly. No wonder he was drawn to this totally inappropriate woman.

Suddenly her little horse stumbled. Carly dipped dangerously sideways and bumped into Zeus. Luc reached out to steady her.

"I'm good," she said, but her eyes were wide behind the sunglasses now knocked askew.

"Yes, you are." His voice dropped deep. The words took on a double meaning. "Very good. And very kind."

Something passed between them then. Something that made him reluctant to remove his hand from her sun-warmed back.

The air grew thick, charged.

A horse blew through his nose, harness jangled and the song of katydids was a constant whirr. Voices rose and fell around them.

He tried to make sense of what was happening. His heart stumbled as surely as her horse had.

"Luc?" she said, her voice bewildered.

Another voice, louder and more demanding, echoed his name.

"Luc. Hold up."

Reluctantly Luc withdrew his hand and looked toward the approaching rider. Pammie Wilson.

The strangely mesmerized moment with Carly dissipated. Along with the rest of the riders, he reined to a halt and waited. Zeus dropped his head to pull at the green grass.

Luc struggled to take his mind off Carly and focus on the other woman.

"I think my horse picked up a stone," Pammie said. "Could you check, please?"

"Of course." Though he questioned her reasons for asking him rather than one of the wranglers, Luc dismounted to examine her sleek bay.

The other riders moved on past, forming a semicircle around the small herd of bawling calves and plodding cows they'd picked up along the way.

Dirk rode over and slipped to the ground beside him. "What do you think?"

"I don't see anything." Luc dropped the hoof to run his hands along the animal's hock. "Nothing here either. Perhaps you should have a look."

After repeating the examination, the cowboy frowned. "I don't see anything either."

"But he was limping," Pammie insisted. "He can't be ridden any farther. I will not be responsible for causing him more injury."

"It could be a tendon," Dirk offered. "Wouldn't want to mess with that."

Luc concurred. If in doubt, opt on the side of caution. Good riding stock was expensive and took a long time to train. Carson didn't need to lose a fine horse like this one.

"Can the ranch be notified to bring out another horse and take this one in for further care?"

"Sure. But Miss Wilson here will be without a pony for a while."

To Luc's dismay, Pammie smiled sweetly and moved to his side. "That's okay. Luc's horse is huge. He can easily carry two riders."

For the briefest of moments Luc wanted to refuse. But Zeus was the largest horse in the party. Common courtesy dictated his answer.

Without a word he remounted and offered Pammie a hand up, seating her behind him. He glanced at Carly. She looked away, but not before he spotted the flicker of disappointment behind her sunglasses.

Pammie wrapped her arms around his waist and leaned into his back. "Now this is more like it."

Luc murmured an automatic response, pondering Carly's expression and the moment of awareness that still buzzed in his blood.

On impulse, he nudged Zeus alongside her small horse. She looked up, eyebrow raised in question. Luc leaned out, placed his hat on her head and cantered away with Pammie clinging to him like a wood tick.

Carly grabbed the teetering hat and battled the childish urge to stick out her tongue at the disappearing pair of riders. She settled for a sneer and a sense of fate. Luc had chatted with her, not asked her to go steady. Guys always liked talking to her. End of story.

Sheesh. She could be such an idiot at times.

Luc's Resistol, a size too big, slid over the tops of her ears. The brim settled low on her forehead.

Men were lunkheads, too. They never seemed to figure out when a woman like Pammie Wilson was playing them. They just smiled and fell right into the game.

She supposed that was the reason men were not interested in her beyond friendship. She didn't know how to play those silly games. And furthermore, she didn't want to know.

Tina Osborne galloped up beside her. "Did you see the way she smirked at you?"

Of course she'd seen it. She'd also seen Pammie wrap her arms around Luc's waist and join her hands right above his belt buckle. More importantly, she'd noted Luc's hand placed protectively over Pammie's when he had kicked Zeus into a trot.

Gag.

Not that she was jealous of Luc's attention to pretty Pammie. Well, maybe a teeny bit, but she warned herself to cease and desist. Luc was way out of her league, probably out of Pammie's league, too, but the woman was pretty and graceful and could ride a horse without bouncing like a rubber ball. The only things on Pammie that bounced were her bosoms. All the wranglers had noticed that right away.

"I don't think it was a smirk, actually," Carly said. "I think the sun was in her eyes."

"I could ride by and knock her off his horse," the teen offered.

The idea tickled Carly more than she wanted to admit. "You would, wouldn't you?"

"Sure. I've kicked a few butts. It would be fun."

Carly couldn't resist the giggle. "Let's not spook the cows."

Tina shrugged. "Whatever."

By the time they arrived at Big Creek, Tina's teenage chatter about boys and music and trendy clothes had taken Carly's mind off her own shortcomings.

Along the way, she'd recentered her purpose. She had a job to do. And she'd done that job by taking plenty of snapshots of Luc and his passenger. So as not to arouse suspicion, she'd taken other shots, too, but most of the pictures would be wonderful stuff to send Count Broussard.

Pushing Luc's hat off her forehead, she followed the small herd of bellowing stray cattle beneath the cool shade next to the creek. They were as eager as she for rest and water.

"I'm starved," Tina announced as she jumped from her horse and handed him off to a waiting cowboy.

"Me, too." Carly slid down Stormy's side and looked around. Her backside felt flat and achy and sorely in need of movement. "I think I'll offer the cook my assistance to see if I can speed up dinner."

Tina grimaced. "I'll pass on that deal." She angled her head to where Luc had dismounted and was lifting Pammie from the saddle. "Sure you don't want me to push her in the creek?"

"And poison the water?" Carly raised her camera, aimed and snapped just as Pammie stumbled against Luc's chest.

"Does she have to be so obvious?" This from a teenager who suddenly went on full female alert. "Omigosh, Dirk is looking this way. I think he needs my help." She gave Carly a one-fingered wave. "Catch ya later."

Carly shook her head as Tina stuck her hands in her belt loops, thrust out her chest and strolled toward the cowboy, who was busy unsaddling horses.

Carly stretched her stiff muscles. She needed to return Luc's hat, but there was no way she'd go near him with Pammie around.

Leaving her horse for the wranglers to attend, she went to the chuck wagon.

The vehicle had come to rest in an open space separated from the creek and its line of spreading oaks and drooping willows by several yards. From the presence of a few crude amenities, Carly figured this was the usual stopping place for the Benedict roundup.

"Need any help?"

A young cowboy, busy pulling items from the wagon, turned her way. "Yes, ma'am. I could use a hand."

He had a thin face, all angles and bones, but his eyes were a pleasant gray.

Carly commanded herself not to look at the oak tree where Luc and Pammie stood talking. "Show me what to do."

"I'll need some firewood."

"You got it." Any number of fallen branches and logs lay scattered along the creek bank and beneath the trees. Carly placed her camera on the wagon ledge for safekeeping and started off in that direction.

Luc's voice winged across the space. "Be alert for rattlesnakes."

Carly froze in her tracks. Very slowly she turned in Luc's direction. "Snakes?"

Pammie laughed. The sound scraped across Carly's nerves like fingernails on a blackboard.

"Just wear your gloves, ma'am," the cook called as he pulled a huge black pot from the wagon. "You'll be fine."

"Gee, that's reassuring." She glanced down at the thin leather riding gloves. What if a rattler had fangs the length of railroad spikes?

The cowboy waved off her concern. "We use this place so often we've likely run all the snakes out of here by now."

"Yeah, you and all the other snake charmers," Carly muttered.

Her sarcasm brought barks of laughter from the two men. Pammie curled her lip in distaste.

Too hungry to let a little thing like a snarling ten-foot

rattlesnake or an equally snarling female come between her and food, Carly shoved Luc's hat down on her head and set to work. If he wanted his hat, he knew where it was.

In less time than she thought possible, the scent of pork chops and fried potatoes filled the evening air. When the cook rattled an old-fashioned triangle and called, "Come and get it," the humans stampeded.

Carly, belly growling, filled her plate and looked around for a place to sit. Logs encircled the campfire, but it was still too hot to sit close, so she wandered down by the creek to sit on a rock. Others shared the same idea and soon boots were stripped away and feet dangled in the cool water.

Carly enjoyed chatting with the irrepressible Tina and a couple from Illinois while two male guests vied for Pammie's attention. At least the blonde wasn't trailing after Luc for the time being.

While the guests ate, the prince helped the wranglers set up camp, leaving his meal for later. She looked up more than once, caught him watching her and experienced a foolish little thrill.

Sheesh. When would she learn?

Darkness lay over the earth like a cozy blanket. The rest of the campers, exhausted from the long afternoon, shuffled in their bedrolls, then lay still. Tree frogs throbbed their rhythmic song and an occasional mosquito buzzed through the smoke and insect repellent. The moon hung orange as an egg yolk in a sky sprinkled with stars.

Luc hunkered beside the campfire, stick in hand,

waiting for the embers to die. He knew better than to leave a fire burning, especially here on a prairie where even an ember could rage out of control so quickly.

They were alone, he and Carly, the only two unable to settle down for the night. Luc realized with not a bit of remorse that he had maneuvered this time alone with her. He didn't know why for certain. Perhaps because he'd felt so good when they'd discussed Philippe and laughed together about the childish prank. He'd thought about that all evening. That and Philippe.

"We can't see stars like this in Dallas," Carly said. She sat on a log, knees together, feet apart, her chin propped on the heel of her hand, staring into the heavens. His stomach dipped at the picture she made.

"Worried about coyotes?" he asked in a low voice, teasing.

"No." When he arched his eyebrows in a pointed look, she shrugged. "Maybe."

"Is that why you are sitting here by the firelight when everyone else is asleep?"

"You're not asleep either." Her hair, which had long since escaped its restraints, fell around her face. She gathered it in one hand and tossed it back. "What's your excuse?"

"Things on my mind. I needed some peace and quiet to think."

"Oh. Sorry." She rose from the log and dusted her behind. "I'll leave you alone then."

She took three steps into the shadows before Luc dropped the stick and called, "Carly, no. Wait."

She pivoted, but he could not read her expression.

"That was not my intent. Please. Don't go on my account." Don't go for any reason. He coveted her company tonight, for reasons he refused to contemplate.

Her hands dived into her back pockets. "I don't want to be a bother."

"Stay." He indicated a plastic package left on a stump. "I'll roast a marshmallow for you."

She smiled and moved back into the dim circle of light to reclaim her seat on the log. "You have something serious on your mind, don't you?"

"Many things." One in particular that he couldn't share even with the kind and compassionate Carly.

"Did talking about Philippe upset you?"

He found a whittled stick and speared several marshmallows onto the shaft.

"No." Yes.

Somewhere in the darkness a calf bawled for its mother and she answered. A spark snapped from the campfire. Luc snuffed it with his boot, then sat down next to Carly and held the marshmallows over the coals.

Carly reached for the stick. "I can do that."

Luc dodged to the side. "*Ma chérie,* you are in the presence of an expert marshmallow chef. Do not interfere with perfection."

"All right, Mr. Chef. If you'll tell me what's bothering you." A hand braced at each side, she stretched her booted feet out in front of her. "I'm a good listener."

Indeed she was. Too good perhaps, dangerously so. But he'd talked to her of Philippe and felt better for it, relieved somehow. Her relaxed posture was an invitation to trust, and his need to unburden proved too strong to resist.

Staring into the glowing embers, he rotated the marshmallows and considered the best approach. If he spoke in terms of business rather than the monarchy, he would not be in danger of revealing too much.

"There are difficulties within my family's business," he said finally, for indeed running a country was a difficult and serious business.

"What kind of difficulties? Is the company in trouble?" Her thigh brushed his as she shifted on the roughened bark.

"Not exactly, although I believe we could do better."

"Then what is it?" Her dark eyes studied him, concerned. He tried not to think about her long legs touching his.

"My brother was to take over as head of the business. Now the role falls to me."

"Why is that a problem?"

He looked at her without saying a word, knowing instinctively that she would understand. She didn't disappoint him.

"Ah, I see." She sat up, angled her body toward him. Her dark eyes shimmered with an unnerving tenderness. "The naughty little boy who wouldn't learn his lessons. You don't think you're up to it."

He hitched a shoulder. "Philippe was trained from birth, groomed to become—" He paused, searching for the words that would tell without revealing. "My father always intended Philippe to take over. He was perfect for the position. I, on the other hand, am not."

An ember popped, sending a curl of smoke into the air. The hickory scent blended pleasantly with the sweet, browning marshmallows. Carly was so close he could hear her quiet breathing, feel the warmth from her body.

"Okay, so we've established your thoughts on that. Is your father a good leader?"

"The best."

"Wait." She laid her fingers on his arm. "I thought Philippe was the best."

"He would have been the perfect replacement when Father retires." Which would be soon.

"Okay. Let me get this straight. Your father is a great leader. Your brother would have been a great leader. Why does that mean that you wouldn't be a great leader, too?"

He tilted his head, blinked at her. Why? Because he wasn't Philippe. He was the second son, the pretender to the throne of Montavia, the undisciplined prince. Or so Count Broussard and any host of other naysayers had intimated.

"There are doubters within the company." He'd almost said *country*.

"Have you done anything to give them reason to doubt you?"

"No." He shrugged and pulled the stick from the fire. "Perhaps when I was younger and more foolish, but not since Philippe's death."

Carly reached for the roasted marshmallows.

"Be careful. They're hot."

Paying him no mind, she took some of the sticky

stuff between her finger and thumb and examined it. "Perfectly browned. You are a chef *magnifique.*"

"*Merci, mademoiselle.* I am a man of many talents."

"Indeed you are." Her lips closed around the marsh-mallows. "Mmm. This is good."

Luc could hardly take his eyes off her mouth. She made matters worse by giving each finger a dainty swipe with her pink tongue.

"Have you studied the business thoroughly?" Her voice was thick with marshmallows.

"What? Oh." He blinked and forced his gaze back to the fire. As serious as their conversation was, he'd almost lost the drift. "Of course I know the business. Inside and out."

"Would you work hard? Give it your best? Do everything you can to make the company flourish?"

"Certainly. If I were…in charge." He'd almost slipped again, almost said if he was king. "I have ideas, plans that could make our business much more profitable and help many people in the process."

"Well, I don't see what the big deal is. I've watched you here on the ranch. You're smart, well educated. You work hard. People listen when you speak and follow your lead. And you're a pretty nice guy." She raised her shoulders. "There you go."

Luc turned the roasting stick sideways and sampled his own cooking while he absorbed her simple wisdom.

Was Carly right? He hoped so. And with that hope, he knew for the first time that he desired to be king. Always before he'd wondered, unable to separate his feelings of inadequacy from his desire. Now he knew.

And he had Carly to thank for that realization. Sweet, endearing Carly.

"These *are* good." His words muffled around the mouthful of marshmallows.

"Danged spiffy they're good. I know the chef." She grinned at him. The white sugary substance clung to her lips.

He stared at her mouth—again. His stomach tightened.

She saw the direction of his gaze and raised a finger. "Do I have—"

"Yes." Before she could flick away the marshmallow, he covered her hand. "Allow me."

He hadn't intended to do anything crazy. But he kept thinking of how much better he felt after talking to her. How her encouragement buoyed him.

He also couldn't get the thought of her lush, beautiful mouth out of his head.

Her hand was soft and warm and very different from his now work-roughened one. And the fingers were sticky. As sticky as her luscious mouth.

Carly sat very still. Her breath puffed tantalizingly against his knuckles.

A battle raged inside him. His feelings made no sense. The woman had listened to him, that was all. She was completely inappropriate.

And at this moment he could not have cared less.

Holding her dark, luminous gaze with his, he raised

her hand to his mouth, rolled his tongue over the smooth skin and then suckled that one sticky finger.

Carly's lips parted. Her chest rose and fell, a fitting partner for his own. Her eyes fluttered shut.

When she sighed, he resisted no more. Using her hand as leverage, he pulled her to him and kissed her.

She tasted the way he'd dreamed—yes, he admitted, he'd thought of this. The sweet marshmallow melted on his tongue as Carly melted against his chest. She made a soft humming sound that electrified him. He deepened the kiss, and the spark of fire ignited deep in his belly. The flames grew brighter and hotter until he thought they would consume the two of them.

Suddenly Carly shoved hard against his chest. He tumbled back and slid from the log, going to his knees in front of her. Her face showed terror.

Shocked at his own loss of control, he reached for her. "Carly. I shouldn't have— Forgive me."

"No, not that." She jabbed a finger urgently over his shoulder. "That."

Pivoting on his toes, he saw that the flames he'd envisioned as passion were all too real.

The wagon was on fire!

Chapter Seven

Flames licked from beneath the canvas top like hungry tongues.

Still reeling from Luc's startling, glorious kiss, Carly leaped from the rough-hewn log and took off in a dead run.

"Carly. Stay back." Luc caught her from behind, wrapped strong arms around her.

"My camera. I left it on the wagon."

His marshmallow-sweet breath puffed against the side of her face. She wanted to turn and kiss him again.

"Forget the camera," he said.

Easy for him to say. His livelihood didn't depend on those pictures. Hers did. But from the looks of the fire, her film was probably long gone. She sagged in his arms. "I'll go for water."

"Alert the cowboys first." And then he thundered away, straight toward the burning wagon.

"Luc," she called, knowing she wasted her breath. Luc would take the lead, as he was born to do, even if the action put him in jeopardy. Silly man. He didn't even know that about himself.

Carly wheeled toward the area beneath the trees where rows of sleeping bags lay like dark mounds. She stuck her fingers between her teeth and whistled.

"Fire!"

The cowboys bolted from their beds. Campers moved much more slowly, confused and disoriented. "What? What's going on?"

"The wagon's on fire," Carly screamed and then wasted no more time. She rushed back to the camp-fire, grabbed the biggest cooking pot and raced to the creek.

Over the buzz of startled voices Luc yelled through the darkness, "Wet some saddle blankets."

In the glow of the burning wagon she saw him battle the growing flames with a bedroll. By now the wranglers raced around, grabbing bedding and anything else that could be used to smother the flames.

Horses, unnerved by the scent of smoke and the commotion, whinnied and moved with restless fear. Cattle bawled.

Carly yanked horse blankets from atop saddles, shoved them into the kettle and filled it with creek water. For once she was glad for her size. The wet blankets and pot were heavy, but she lugged them back to the wagon.

As she stumbled into the circle of light, a hand reached out. Luc, his handsome face strained with effort and flushed from the heat. "I'll take that."

He handed off the wet blankets to the waiting wranglers, then went back to work. The slap of wet wool blended with the crackle of burning wood.

Luc seemed to be everywhere at once, calling out orders, organizing.

"Dirk, see to the fire in the grass. Jack, move those horses further back. Heck, give me a hand here. Everyone else, fill anything available with water."

Yet he never stopped fighting the fire. He was a guest, just as she was, but he was closer than anyone to the burning wagon. For a royal raised in the lap of luxury, he showed no fear.

What if he got hurt? Fighting fire would not be on Count Broussard's list of safe activities.

Luc should let the wranglers put out the flames. But telling him would do no good. Luc would do what he thought was right.

Arms aching, Carly carted more water from the creek. Just as she stepped into the fire-lit perimeter, Dirk came charging around the back of the wagon.

"Where's Willie?" The red glow lighting the night emphasized his fear. "Has anybody seen Willie?"

The young cook was nowhere to be seen.

The front of the vehicle was engulfed by now, and smoke formed a dense cloud around the back.

"Oh, dear heaven," one of the women cried. "He must be in the wagon."

All eyes, wide with horror, stared toward the flaming

conveyance. One arched truss snapped and fell. Sparks shot high into the night sky.

Carly was mortified that she'd thought of her camera instead of the young cook. But who could have guessed he'd sleep inside on such a warm night?

Before anyone else had time to react, Luc shoved a pillowcase into Carly's kettle, wrapped the wet cloth around his face and raced toward the opening in the back of the wagon.

"Luc, no!" Carly started after him but found herself manacled between Dirk and Heck. Luc disappeared into the smoke.

"You stay put, Miss Carly," Dirk said, his soot-streaked face grim. "Nothing you can do."

The canvas top of the wagon was all but gone. The wood frame cracked and groaned as the front crumpled and flames spread to the wheels. A hush fell over the campers as they fell back, unable to bear the heat any longer.

Carly's eyes stung from the smoke, her throat ached.

Like a living thing, fear snaked up her spine, hissed inside her brain.

Only five minutes ago Luc had been kissing her. Now his life was in danger.

Time crawled. Seconds passed. Then minutes.

Carly knew she should go for more water. She should keep battling the blaze. But she couldn't. Not now. Not when Luc was in danger.

She pressed two shaky fingers to her mouth. The sweet taste of marshmallows and Luc's lips had become smoke and ashes.

Suddenly two dark forms stumbled from the boiling smoke. The smaller one visibly sagged against the other.

"Luc." Thank goodness. Oh, thank goodness. Her knees threatened to buckle, but she forced them to remain upright. Luc was strong. She had to be strong, as well. No one had time for hysteria.

Dirk rushed forward to lighten the load from Luc's shoulders. Willie's harsh cough ripped the night, heralding the glad news that he was alive.

"Air. He needs air." The campers parted. Mr. Osborne, carrying a lantern, led the way to the creek, where his wife quickly spread a blanket for the young cook. The others went back to the fire fight.

Luc staggered into the clearing. He leaned forward, hands on his knees, gasping for fresh air. His face was dirty and streaked, his eyes red and tearing, his clothes disheveled in a way Carly had never seen.

He looked wonderful.

The next morning, when Carly stumbled down to a late breakfast, the dining room was abuzz with talk of the fire and of Luc's heroic rescue.

Carly had planned to sleep until noon, but she'd hardly slept at all. After she and the other guests had been transported back to the ranch at midnight, the campout abandoned, her thoughts had rolled like the flickering images of an old home movie. The kiss. The fire. The fear. Fear of losing what was not hers to lose—and never would be. A bad-boy prince who wasn't bad at all. A real hero so far out of her reach she must be delusional.

Carly wanted to despair over her camera but couldn't. She was too thankful that no one had been seriously injured.

If only she hadn't left the expensive Canon on the wagon.

She sighed and slid into the chair next to Tina Osborne. No use crying over spilled milk.

Luc's place remained empty, as did those of Carson and Teddi Benedict.

Disappointment descended. Silly, foolish, but undeniable. She'd wanted to see Luc, to reaffirm that he was all right and to gaze once more into the eyes she'd drowned in last night before the fire had begun.

Over and over she relived that moment when Luc's lips had settled upon hers. She'd felt like a princess in a fairy tale. Like Cinderella. For that fraction of time, before the fire had shocked her into reality, she'd believed in the impossible.

Luc had kissed her out of gratitude or friendship or some such thing. Certainly not out of attraction or— dare she think it?—love.

A little shiver went through her at the word. *Love*. Had she ever felt this way before? Could one kiss make her fall in love with a handsome prince? Or had she been falling all along and been too focused on her work to realize it?

She dived for the coffee carafe and knocked over the salt shaker in the process. Righting it, she poured a hot, fragrant cup of java and sipped. She had to stop thinking the L word. Carly the Klutz could not fall in love. Especially with the unreachable crown prince of

Montavia—her ticket back to Dallas and her future as a private investigator.

Time to let her intellect and not her emotions take control. She had a commitment to fulfill with Count Broussard. Firmly she thrust Luc's kiss and her jumbled emotions into the back of her brain and shut a mental door.

"Where is everybody?" she asked.

"Everybody? Or Luc?"

Carly ignored Tina's pointed question. With studied casualness she took a slice of toast and smeared it with blackberry jam. "Any word on Willie?"

"The boy's fine. Just a little smoke." Mr. Osborne forked a bite of pancake, his double chin quivering with the effort. "The hospital is releasing him this morning. That's where the Benedicts are."

"Mr. Gardner, too, from what the receptionist told me," said Mrs. Osborne. "Said he sat up with Willie all night."

"Oh, hey, I almost forgot." Tina blotted orange juice from black-lined lips. "I found your camera last night."

"You what? You have my camera?" Carly had feared the Canon was gone for good—and her perfect pictures of Luc along with it.

Tina's kohl-rimmed eyes widened. "You're not mad, are ya? I just forgot about it. I saw it lying on the wagon and started to bring it to you, but you were making fish eyes at Luc. Then Willie got hurt and all…."

Having the camera saved from destruction had to be a sign. A sign that Carly was to do her job and stop focusing on one little, meaningless kiss. Sheesh. You'd think she'd never locked lips with anyone before.

Carly gave Tina's shoulders a hug. She was actually starting to like the girl. "Tina, I owe you one."

"Cool. 'Cause I wanna ride into town with you today. I'm dying to go shopping."

"How did you know I was going to town?"

Tina wagged her eyebrows. "Heard you tell your honey when the two of you were getting all chummy around the campfire."

Just how much had the girl seen? Carly was afraid to ask.

"He is not my honey." But she couldn't deny that for a wrinkle in time last night she'd entertained that fantasy.

"Whatever. Since you're not mad, I gotta tell ya something else."

Carly took another hit of the strong black coffee and braced for bad news.

"Mama made me stay back from the fire. So I thought what the hey, catch the excitement on film—you know? So I snapped some pics. Is that okay?"

Carly wanted to shout hallelujah. She couldn't have Luc, but she still had her camera and some incredible photos to send to her current employer.

On second thought, the count might not be too happy about Luc getting that close to danger. But her job was to record and report, not pass judgment.

"Very okay. And if your parents agree, you can definitely ride into town with me. I need to do some shopping myself—for some decent shoes."

An eerie sensation trickled into her consciousness. Shoes? She wanted new shoes?

She crunched into her half-eaten toast as if it were full of worms. She wanted shoes?

But it was true. She, who had shied away from any form of shopping all her life, had the undeniable urge to buy a pair of shoes. Pretty shoes. Flirty shoes.

Now where had that foreign concept come from?

Tina clasped her hands over her heart in an exaggerated groan of ecstasy as they entered a trendy little boutique in Maribella's one and only strip mall.

Carly laughed. "Do you always drool at the sight of purses and low-rider pants?"

Tina stroked her fingers over a rack of shiny camisoles. "Yeah, I do. Don't you?"

"Not usually." But she had to admit the idea of a new outfit appealed more than she'd ever imagined. And she could use a swimsuit, too. Ever since arriving at the guest ranch she'd wanted to try out the Olympic-size pool but hadn't brought a suit.

She began a slow perusal of the shop's selections. Besides an assortment of pretty tops, pants and skirts, there was a nice array of accessories. And shoes. Lots of shoes. And not one pair of brogans.

This was her sister's kind of store. The kind of place Carly normally avoided the way ten-year-old boys avoid baths. Why try to make a silk purse out of a sow's ear, as the saying went. She was too tall and too gawky and too clumsy to wear pretty shoes.

But for reasons she couldn't comprehend, Carly

wandered over to the shoes, sat down on the small bench and pulled off her hiking boots. Tina disappeared into a dressing room with an armful of clothing.

One particular pair of heels, ridiculous and impractical, captured her attention. Heels. She was too tall for heels.

But she tried them on anyway.

"Oh, my." She turned her foot this way and that, admiring the sassy, strappy open-toed slings.

Wonder what an ankle bracelet would look like with these?

Tina popped out of the dressing room wearing a scanty silver acrylic tube top.

"What do you think of this—" She took one look at Carly's feet and squealed. "They're perfect. You gotta buy them and get rid of those ugly boot things."

Feeling a little silly, Carly stood. She towered over the teen.

"I'm too tall."

Tina tossed her head in the look teenagers reserve for the ultrastupid. "Duh. That's the whole point. When you're tall, you accentuate the fact. Like runway models do. Just look at you. You have such pretty slim feet and your legs are gorgeous."

"I'll trip and kill myself—or worse, kill somebody else."

"You will not. Wearing heels takes a little practice, but you can do it."

"Yeah. Like brain surgery takes a little practice."

But she walked around on the carpeted area and didn't stumble once. She teetered a couple of times, but she didn't go down like a piano dropped from the third story. In fact, she moved with far more grace in the heels than she ever did in her boots. Amazing.

"But I need practical shoes, not fancy heels."

Tina pulled a face. "What you need is serious help. Don't you know the rules of shopping? Buy the heels for dress and get another pair for every day. Get two pair. And I'll do your toenails for you."

Her budget was already strained. She didn't need shoes at all.

"Here." Tina thrust a pair of black flats into her hand. "Try these."

This was nuts. She didn't shop.

But she did. In the next hour, with Tina pushing like a salesman on commission, Carly tried on shoes and tops and skirts and swimsuits. Tina did the same.

When she walked out of the dressing room with a slit-side georgette skirt swirling around her knees and the snazzy heels on her feet, she felt more feminine than she ever had in her life. Funny how being kissed by a prince made a woman think about such things.

"Wow. You look hot."

A giggle bubbled up in her throat. She felt hot. Now how stupid was that?

She had to get hold of herself. Trying on clothes was more fun than she remembered, but buying them was a waste of time and money. She was the brain, not the beauty. Men wouldn't find her attractive if she was iron filings and they were magnets.

Whatever she'd imagined in Luc's eyes and in his kiss was just that. Imaginary.

Get over yourself, Carly.

Oddly disappointed, she resolved to change back into her real clothes and stop playing dress-up. She'd taken two steps when Carson and Teddi Benedict entered the shop.

Somehow she didn't figure Carson as a boutique kind of guy.

The brother and sister came directly toward her.

"We thought that was your car out front." Teddi gave her a quick hug, leaving behind the scent of plumeria. "Carson wanted to make sure you were all right after the craziness last night."

"What a nice thing to do. As you can see, I'm fine." Clearly addle-brained from smoke inhalation but otherwise functional. "How's Willie?"

"Good. Out of the hospital. His folks took him home with them for a few days. But he'll be fine."

"I'm glad. Any word on how the fire started?"

Teddi cast a cautious glance at her brother. "Willie admitted he was smoking in the wagon and dozed off."

Carson's expression darkened. "It's against the rules. If all of you hadn't taken charge the way you did, we could have had a real disaster on our hands."

"Luc was the one who took charge." The words tumbled out. "We just followed his lead."

Carson's frown grew even deeper and Carly knew why. A crown prince shouldn't have been placed in such danger.

She couldn't resist asking, "Luc is okay, isn't he?"

"Safe and sound in bed, catching up on the rest he

missed last night," Teddi said. Her amber gaze suddenly registered Carly's attire. "Say, you look smashing."

Carly barely heard the compliment. She was in the throes of a vision. Luc, golden hair touseled on a pillow, muscular chest naked—for she was certain he'd sleep sans shirt.

Tina appeared at her side in a startlingly indecent pair of short shorts that displayed her belly button and butt cheeks. "I told her she looks great, but she won't listen to me."

"A new wardrobe is not in my budget right now, I'm afraid." Carly bent to remove the heels.

A masculine hand touched her arm. "Keep them."

Startled, Carly gazed into Carson Benedict's dark eyes. "Pardon?"

"Buy the blasted shoes. The skirt, too. It looks good." Carson was probably the only man on the planet who could sound angry giving a compliment. "Put them on my charge card."

Now she was more than startled. "I don't think so."

"It's the least I can do. To make up for your bad experience last night."

Bad experience? Last night was the best night of her life. Part of it, anyway.

"Do it, Carly." Teddi gave an impish grin and in a stage whisper said, "Carson isn't usually this generous."

"No compensation necessary. I can buy these things for myself." What else could she do with Cranky Carson glowering so?

"Good." The dark Benedict spun on his boot heel and headed toward the exit without another word.

His sister gave a happy shrug and followed. At the door she whirled, favoring them with a jaunty two-handed wave.

"That was weird," Tina said, staring after the brother and sister as they disappeared out onto the street.

As she headed into the dressing room to change, Carly thought the same thing. Lots of things were weird about the Benedicts, but she couldn't quite put her finger on the reasons. If she weren't already gainfully employed by Count Broussard, she'd do some checking on the pair.

Count Broussard! She'd almost forgotten her purpose in coming to town in the first place. This was nuts. She had to get a grip. She was so wrapped up in shopping and daydreams of the handsome prince that she'd almost gone back to the ranch without those pictures.

How was she possibly going to spend the rest of the summer spying on the man who had turned her usually brilliant mind to thoughts of sexy sandals and toenail polish?

Chapter Eight

The telephone woke Luc from an erotic dream. He struggled against the sound, wanting to stay wrapped in Carly's long legs, but the phone was insistent. He pawed at it, knocked the receiver from the base and fumbled to pull it against his ear.

"Hullo." Smoke and sleep had turned his voice raspy.

"Luc." The single word from his father jerked him fully awake.

"Father? Is something wrong?" He pushed the rumpled sheet off his legs and sat up.

"Precisely the same question I have for you." King Alexandre spoke in the flowing Montavian French.

"Sir?" Luc replied in kind. There was no way his father could be calling about the fire. "I'm afraid I don't understand."

"I hope that is true. But I must ask you to explain the rather unflattering photographs that have begun circulating in the tabloids."

"Of me? There can't be."

"There are. And they are all recent photos, not old ones. You need a haircut badly."

Luc raked a hand over the unruly mass of waves. Father thought his hair lacked royal decorum. If the king hadn't sounded so concerned, Luc would have laughed.

Instead he sighed wearily. Even when he was out of the country the press refused to give him any peace. He was thousands of miles away and still they used his face to sell newspapers. After the ugly innuendos surrounding Philippe's death, Luc loathed them. But the Jardine family had learned to ignore the yellow journalism, so why was the king concerned this time?

"Most likely they are pictures from the grand regatta. Probably nothing to worry about."

"No, my son." The king's voice softened to polished steel. It was the tone he used in council meetings that made every member sit up and take notice. "There are allegations of unsavory behavior unbecoming a future king. Behaviors that could keep your bid for the throne from being approved by the Grand Council. Need I remind you no one wants an undisciplined king?"

Ah. So the press had gone beyond their usual tactics.

"Sir, I assure you I am guiltless. Other than my computer work for the palace and the tourism department, my days are spent with Carson and his horses. I'm learning a great deal about running an establishment of this sort. Knowledge that could be useful to our country."

No need for the king to know about Carly. She had nothing to do with the unsavory paparazzi.

But he felt a little guilty for leaving her out of the conversation. She most definitely occupied a large portion of his days—and if his dream was any indication, a major part of his nights, as well.

That one kiss from Carly's beautiful, lush mouth had shifted his world. He feared he was losing the battle to remember that she was unsuitable. Not that he'd ever cared much about that sort of thing to begin with.

He heard his father's slow intake of breath and the equally slow exhale. "All right. Your word is enough for me. I only wish I knew how to stop this kind of thing before public opinion is swayed and the damage becomes irreversible."

The photos troubled Luc, as well. Some contingent of Montavian society still believed him responsible in some way for Philippe's untimely death, though no one dared say it to his face. But if he was judged incompetent or unfit for whatever reason, the throne could pass out of the direct line of King Alexandre.

"Scan and e-mail the prints to me. I want to see if I can discern where they were taken and when."

"The paparazzi doesn't matter as long as the Grand Council knows that their allegations are untrue. That's difficult to do with you in America. I don't need to tell you that Arturo is in a frenzy."

His chief advisor was a brilliant man, deeply committed to the royal family and vastly knowledgeable of

Montavian government, but Luc dreaded returning to
his subtle hints that Philippe would have made a better
king. He knew that.

In truth, he wasn't ready to leave America for other
reasons, as well. And yes, he admitted, his reluctance
had much to do with the charming American. "Shall I
come home, then?"

"Soon perhaps. Sooner if this slander continues."

"Agreed. Whenever you say the word. But in the
meantime, Father, I want to see those photos."

"You know how I feel about computers." The king
had never so much as learned to turn one on. "But I will
try to find someone trustworthy to e-mail copies to
you."

"Thank you, sir."

And then the conversation turned personal, to family
and court business.

By the time he hung up the phone, he had almost put
the tabloids out of his mind.

Almost.

Legs crossed, Carly sat on the bed sifting through
the latest developed snapshots of His Royal Highness
Prince Luc of Montavia.

She had to admit there were some dandy shots.

"Good golly, Miss Molly," she murmured, doing
her level best not to drool on the prints. No wonder the
European press hounded him.

She started two stacks. One to send to Count Broussard and a few for her own professional records.

Oh, heck, who was she kidding? One stack was for

herself. Trouble was, the keeper stack grew larger by the minute.

Here was a shot of the time they'd walked down to the stables. She had whistled through her teeth and Luc had said she was refreshing. The memory washed through her, all warm and fuzzy. *Refreshing,* he'd said, and that simple word had made her feel special. Though innocuous enough to share with her employer, she couldn't bear to turn loose of that one.

She scribbled the date and the memory on the back of the photo and laid it on her pillow with others.

As the next captured moment came into focus, Carly's smile changed to a grimace. Luc and perfect Pammie at the campsite. The woman flirted outrageously with the prince, and darn his hide, he looked to be enjoying every second. The pinch of jealousy she'd suffered had been far too unpleasant.

She put that one in a separate pile, facedown. Count Broussard could have it and any others like it.

But then came the pictures Tina had snapped of the fire. Carly flipped through them, her stomach heavy with remembered horror. Luc battling the flames. Luc carting the limp Willie from the burning wagon.

Perhaps sharing those with the count was not the wisest course of action. If the palace discovered the crown prince had been in jeopardy, they would insist he return to Montavia or allow his bodyguards to come to the ranch. Luc didn't want that.

Neither did she.

There had to be other photos suitable for submission to the royal advisor.

She looked at another. And then another. By the end of the stack, she groaned. Photos of Luc laughing, roasting marshmallows, riding the gleaming black horse, were spread across her bed like a photo essay. She didn't want to share any of them. They were too personal, each one a memory of something she had grown to love about her dream prince.

"Get a grip, Carly."

Dream prince was the right description. He was a fantasy, and she was mooning around like the love-starved Tina. In a few weeks Luc would be back in his country, she would return to Dallas—and unless she handled this job properly, her days would be spent in the unemployment line.

Enough thoughts of romantic interludes with a fairy-tale prince.

Other than a handful of photos and the memory of one glorious kiss, her career would be the only thing left when Luc went home to Montavia. And she would do well to focus on the future, not the impossible. Regardless of her growing feelings, she would do her job.

Besides, if Luc knew of her duplicity—that she was invading his treasured privacy for the sake of gain—he would hate her.

With heavy heart and self-derision she kept only the fire photos and prepared the others to go to Montavia. Then she flipped open the laptop and continued the chronicle of Luc's activities to include with the pictures.

She read back over last night's entry. The piece read like a teenage diary.

His tawny hair glistened in the sunlight and the

*smell of his cologne circled about me as he played the
gentleman, hoisting me into the saddle. The touch of his
hands at my waist had my heart thundering louder
than a stampede of a thousand horses. And his smile...*

With a moan of despair Carly dropped her head back
and stared at the rotating ceiling fan. When had she
gone from professional documentation to writing a romance novel?

She was in deep. Very deep.

This prince guy, with his polished manners, his deep
intellect and his genuine humanity wreaked havoc with
her emotions—and her career. She couldn't be in love.
She couldn't.

But she was. Carly the Klutz had fallen hard and fast
for a living, breathing prince.

What an absolutely idiotic thing to do. Even if Luc
returned her feelings, nothing could come of a relationship between them. Didn't royals have to marry other
royals? Wouldn't he likely be betrothed from birth to
some blue-blooded Montavian blonde who'd never
stumbled over a flowerpot in her life?

A knock at the door had her slamming the lid on the
purple prose. No one—absolutely no one—on the
planet could ever read the embarrassing journal.

"Who is it?"

"Luc."

Her stomach did that weird thing again, as though
she'd jumped off the high diving board. Frantically she
stashed the photos under her pillow and shoved the
computer onto the nightstand.

Luc. What did he want? Oh, who was she kidding?

She didn't care what he wanted. After spending an entire day without one glimpse of him, she was just thrilled to have him here.

On the way to the door she paused to thump her head against the wall three times. Idiot. Fool. Imbecile.

And then, heart thudding, she yanked the door open and tried to play it cool.

"Hi."

He smiled, and there she went again, pulse hammering, stomach jumping.

"I thought I heard a thump. Are you all right?"

No. She was not all right. She was mentally incompetent.

"I was, uh, tidying up a bit." Hoo boy, when had she begun talking like a reject from a British finishing school? "What's up?" That was better. Now if her insides would stop quivering with delight.

"Would you care to have a swim?" he asked. "The pool is usually empty at this time."

And he was, no doubt, a world-class swimmer. Probably had swum the English Channel a few dozen times. "Gonna show me some fancy strokes?"

Oops. That didn't come out right.

"Diving is my forte."

"Ah, that forte thing again. Well, it just so happens that I know a dive or two myself."

The corners of his eyes crinkled. "Do I hear a challenge?"

"Yes, you do." What the heck? In for a penny, in for a pound. "A pool of cool water sounds good after last night's fire."

His expression sobered. "Absolutely. I've no wish to do that again any time soon."

Carly leaned her cheek against the doorjamb. "What you did for Willie was incredibly courageous." She'd been wanting to tell him that.

"A necessity." Luc shrugged off the compliment. "The others would have done the same."

She didn't bother to express the obvious—they hadn't.

But the frightening fire was not a subject she wanted to revisit today, so she said, "Just so happens I bought a new swimsuit today. I'm dying to try it out."

"Then we must give an appropriate debut to your latest fashion acquisition."

Carly stifled a giddy giggle. Sometimes he talked so cute. "Works for me. How about if I bring my camera and let you take my picture. Me in a bikini. My sister won't believe it."

Neither did she. Part of being a good P.I. was making the most of an opportunity, and she should be happy to have such a smooth excuse to bring along her camera. Somehow, though, manipulating a man she cared for didn't feel right. And the last thing she wanted was photos of herself.

"A bikini?" Luc's eyebrows lifted in teasing speculation. "I would be delighted."

Well, that would make exactly one of them. She was horrified. Horrified to wear the new bathing suit. Horrified at her jumbled emotions.

Everything was getting too complicated. Her feelings for Luc warred with her need to succeed at the only thing she was good at. She didn't know whether she had agreed to the swim for business or for pleasure. But she suspected it might be the latter—and wrong—reason.

"Great." She swiped the camera from the bedside table and pushed it into his hand. "Let me change and I'll meet you at the pool in ten minutes."

"Sounds like a plan." With a quick smile and a tilt of his head he took the camera and started down the hall.

Carly almost giggled again. Luc absorbed American expressions the way a biscuit absorbs gravy. She tried her best not to watch him walk away, but the sight of the crown prince of Montavia dressed in formfitting jeans and cowboy shirt was too good to resist. In truth, Luc would have all her attention no matter who or what he was.

To her chagrin, he turned and caught her staring. One eyebrow hiked upward and an amused grin wreathed his face. "Ten minutes?"

Feeling the heat wash over her cheekbones, she nodded like an idiot and slunk back inside the room to change. So she'd been caught looking at his behind. Big deal. Let him think she was hot for him. She wasn't.

Okay, so she was. He didn't know, couldn't know, that she wanted a great deal more from him than his gorgeous body.

Five minutes later Carly headed toward the pool house, tugging at the top of her bathing suit. Whatever had possessed her to buy a bikini? Her underwear covered more than this.

But terrible Tina and the relentless salesclerk had insisted she looked sexy and beautiful in it. When had she ever cared about either of those attributes? She was gawky Carly Carpenter who only attracted men with peanuts for brains or those who thought she would put out just to have a date.

But today she hardly remembered that insecure woman. She *felt* pretty, sexy.

A real live prince was waiting. A prince of a guy that had stolen her heart. And for this one moment in time she could pretend to be Cinderella…until the clock struck midnight.

Luc trod across the dewy grass and entered the warm, humid swimming area, lost in thoughts of an earlier conversation with Carson Benedict. He had told his friend that his stay was coming to an end, that he was needed in Montavia. Curiously the usually supportive Carson had urged him to remain a while longer, to relax and let the troublesome press take care of itself. Carson had even been the one to suggest the swim with Carly.

Not that he was complaining.

"Trying to fix me up?" Luc had asked, half joking.

Instead of returning his laugh, Carson had frowned. "Won't hurt you to enjoy a pretty woman, take your mind off your problems for a while."

His old friend was right about that. The last twenty-four hours had been stressful. He was grateful that no harm had come to the young cook or to any of Carson's guests. And after the kiss he had shared with Carly, he realized there was something there. With the obligations and expectations of an entire country weighing on him, he wasn't sure what to do about it.

Towel over one shoulder, he walked around the edge of the pool, tested the water with his foot and then sat on the end of a lounge chair to wait for his impromptu date. If Carson hadn't suggested it, he probably would have asked her on his own.

Carly was a beguiling puzzle. Awkward, brilliant, wise and funny. He liked her very much. If only… He shook the thought away. There were no *if onlys*. There was just the reality of his situation. A crown prince soon to assume the monarchy had to have the love and trust and respect of his people. His rowdy youth had raised more than one Montavian eyebrow. Raising more would embarrass his family and damage his chances of a smooth transition when Father retired.

He couldn't do that to his family or his country. No matter how much he enjoyed Carly's companionship, he was committed to finding a woman with the proper lineage—someday.

But he was here now. Someday was in the future.

A woman's tall, shadowy form approached the Plexiglas door. Pleasant anticipation winged through him.

The door scraped open and she stepped inside. The sense of anticipation gave way to something more powerful, more significant. All the breath whooshed out of him. He was thankful to be sitting, because a royal did not make social blunders by collapsing at the sight of a beautiful woman.

And Carly Carpenter was exquisite. Hadn't he fantasized about those legs? And wondered about her body?

As he had long suspected, those horrid baggy shirts and pants had been hiding a treasure.

To regain his composure, Luc lifted the small camera, located her in the viewfinder and snapped. At the flash of light, Carly spotted him.

"Hey. No fair. Give a girl some warning. I had my eyes closed."

Thankfully his were wide open.

She came toward him, long, glorious legs striding with the elegance of a runway model, dark hair swinging above ample breasts. He snapped again.

"Your new swimsuit is very becoming." That was the understatement of the year. He felt like a schoolboy at Eton, thick-tongued and sweaty palmed.

The compliment didn't make her preen as most women of his acquaintance would do. Instead she seemed to curl up, trying to hide in the limited bits of cherry-red material.

"Thank you."

Shy. Another enchanting facet of his Carly.

His own thoughts startled him. *His* Carly? He had a country full of women to choose from and yet this disarmingly self-conscious creature captivated him more than any female ever had.

"You are stunning. Don't hide." Laying aside the camera, he rose, pulled her crossed arms away from her body and held them out to each side to admire her. She was more than stunning, more even than he'd imagined. He was already enamored of her personality, but now he had to deal with a surging libido.

A blush started at her toes and worked its way to the roots of her hair.

Luc laughed. "It's nice to be proven correct."

A little shiver sent charming gooseflesh down her arms. "Excuse me?"

"I knew you would look lovely."

Carly stepped away from his hold and recrossed her arms. "You must have inhaled too much smoke last night. Your thinking is addled."

The woman had no idea that she was fascinating. What could be more appealing to a man than that? He wanted to kiss her again, to find out if her mouth truly tasted as sweet as he remembered.

He moved toward her, feeling powerful and aggressive. He knew how to get what he wanted from a woman. He always had.

But what exactly was it that he wanted from this one? Kisses, yes. But something more? Something deeper?

The thought should have given him pause, but he ignored the warning bells. He wanted to kiss her, hold her, touch her. That was all. A normal male response to an attractive female.

Carly must have sensed his intent because she bolted toward the pool and executed a graceful dive off the side. A soft spray of water moistened his feet.

A strange energy, a playful excitement he hadn't felt in too long rose in Luc. He watched until Carly's dark head broke the water and she bobbed to the surface. He shot her a cocky salute.

Then he shocked them both with a cannonball.

She was laughing hysterically when he surfaced.

Treading water, he shoved his hair off his forehead and pretended insult. "Was that not a perfect ten?"

"Oh, it was ten, all right. Ten feet of tidal wave that all but emptied the pool."

"Ah, success. My brother and I often competed for the title of cannonball champion." He hadn't thought of that in years, but the memory warmed him. "Philippe always won."

It was the only sport—if he could call it that—in which Philippe had reigned supreme. Brotherly competition had been fierce in every realm. In the end, that competitive spirit had cost Philippe his life.

Carly hauled her long, slender body, water sluicing off in sheets, up the ladder. As her feet made splish-splash sounds against the concrete, she tugged at the narrow strip of fabric covering her backside.

Luc followed her movement, mesmerized by her grace. He'd seen her stumble and bumble on land, but around the water she was a sylph.

She smoothed one hand over dark slicked-back hair. More water dripped from the ends. The grin she shot him was devilish. "You want competition, mister, you got it."

Then with a yell worthy of a warrior heading into battle, she raced toward the pool, sailed high into the air and rolled into a ball moments before smacking the water. The resulting spray splashed the lounge chairs and sides of the enclosure.

He laughed out loud. If only he'd had her camera at that moment. What a shot.

She popped up directly in front of him, grinning. "How was that?"

"I bow to your excellence."

Carly laughed; droplets hung from her eyelashes. "Dang spiffy, you do. You've met your match." As soon as the words were out, she colored and quickly amended. "I meant you've met your match in the cannonball."

"I understood your intention." But the idea of her being his match in anything at all rolled round and round in his head. "And if it's competition you're after…" He hitched his chin toward the side, indicating a race.

Mischief sparkled in espresso-colored eyes. One soggy finger jabbed at him. "You're on."

Taking the advantage, she flipped over and stroked away.

Pure pleasure such as Luc had not experienced in a long time set his blood to humming. Somewhere along the way, since Philippe's death, he'd lost his joie de vivre. Carly Carpenter had given it back to him.

With a powerful lunge he gave chase, catching her from behind as they approached the shallow end.

Grasping her waist, he thrust her out of the water, high into the air. "You lose."

She placed her hands on his shoulders and grinned down at him, dripping. "Pretty strong picking up an Amazon like me."

"You weigh nothing at all." To prove his point, he lowered her slowly, took her weight first against his chest and then, pressing her close, slid her body down his.

By the time her feet hit bottom, he was breathing hard, though not from exertion.

She stood in the waist-deep water, her hands on his shoulders, her eyes wide and luminous. Few women came close to his height, but Carly was nearly eye level. He liked that. He bit back a groan. He liked everything about this charming lady.

Though Luc knew a relationship could lead to nothing, he was compelled to kiss her. The attraction between them was too strong to deny.

He traced a rivulet of water down one cheek to her lips. Her lush mouth dropped open so that the gentle puff of her breath grazed his water-cooled fingers. Her dark, exotic eyes watched him, curious and a little afraid.

Tenderness gripped him. He didn't want to her to be afraid.

"Carly," he said. And then he kissed her. Her warm, water-slick lips were every bit as wonderful as he'd recalled.

Carly shuddered once and melted into him, every cell in her body yearning for his touch. She loved his lips on hers, his strong hands at her waist, his athletic body aligned with her softer one. Her hands, as if they had a will of their own, roamed his bare, wet back.

Carly, Carly, Carly, her conscience chanted. You're in over your head. He's a prince, for crying out loud. And you're a…nobody.

With reluctance she backed away from Luc's magical mouth. When she found her voice, she quipped, "You kiss pretty good for a foreigner."

One corner of those perfect lips tilted upward, but

desire burned in eyes that matched the pool. "You kiss pretty good for a Texan." He reached for her. "Want to try another? A blend of two cultures perhaps?"

She bobbed backward away from him. If he kissed her again right this minute, she might do something really stupid—like admit she was falling in love with him.

Wouldn't that go over like a pregnant pole-vaulter?

"Maybe later. First I want to see that fancy dive of yours."

"You already have."

"What?" And then she realized his meaning. "The cannonball? That's your best dive?"

Grinning and a bit cocky, he climbed out of the pool. "Maybe not."

While his long strides covered the distance to the diving board, Carly found a towel, spread it in a dry spot and sat down to admire the view. Luc in loose swimming trunks was Adonis reincarnated.

Nah, Adonis could never have looked so good. Nor could he have been such a terrific human being.

She propped her hands behind her and tilted back to watch him. He stood at the end of the diving board, bounced twice and catapulted into the air. Grabbing his ankles in a tuck position, Luc executed two breathtaking somersaults, then stretched to vertical and sliced the water.

Carly shoved two fingers in her mouth and whistled like a maniac.

Luc popped to the surface, shaking the hair and water out of his eyes. "How was that?"

"I gave it a nine-point-two-five."

"Impressed you, didn't I?"

"Yes, but don't let it go to your head. You aren't the only one who can dive."

A slow, sexy smile eased across his gorgeous face. "Show me what you've got."

And so she did. For the next half hour they tried to outdo each other with aerial gymnastics that probably could have killed them both. Occasionally worry tried to intrude—the worry that Luc could get hurt, that she was deceiving him with every picture she snapped, that he would hate her. But in the end, she put them all aside for another time.

Tonight was hers. Luc was hers. She'd worry about the rest tomorrow.

Chapter Nine

"After this latest news, I fear I have no choice. I must return to Montavia right away."

Luc sat in Carson Benedict's upstairs office, hands dangling between his knees as he shared his latest worry. His father had called again. This time the concern was more intense than it had been a week ago. Someone was intentionally trying to discredit the crown prince by filling the media with photos of him in compromising situations. Insinuations that he was out of control buzzed through the kingdom. King Alexandre and the Montavian Grand Council were deeply troubled.

Carson leaned against the long mahogany desk and worried a pen between his fingers. "Who would want to keep you from becoming king?"

"I don't know," Luc said tiredly. "That's what I have to find out. Father has asked an aide to scan the news

photos into the computer and send them to me." The
first pictures that arrived from the palace had been too
vague to be helpful. He'd had a drink in one hand. The
other had been on an unmentionable part of a woman
whose face was blotted out. The tabloid was "protect-
ing the woman's privacy," a claim that infuriated him,
especially since he had no idea who the dark-haired
female was. "Perhaps they will give me a better idea.
And he's asked the royal advisor to investigate. Unfor-
tunately the damage is done. All I can do now is go
home and try to set things straight. My very absence
fuels the speculations."

Carson paced from one side of the long Victorian
room to the other, the usual dark scowl creasing his
forehead. Luc wondered if his old friend ever had any
fun these days. If he even remembered the kind of invigorating conversations and stunning kisses a man
could share with a woman. The kind he had had with
Carly every day since the fire.

He ached to think of leaving her.

As if he read Luc's mind, Carson whipped around
and pointed a finger. "What about Carly?"

Surprise made Luc ask, "What about her?"

"The two of you seem pretty tight."

Anyone on the ranch would have noticed that they
spent a great deal of time together. "She's a special
woman."

"Then why not take her with you? For a visit, I mean."

Luc blinked. Was his interest in Carly that obvious?

Not that he hadn't thought of asking her to go along.
To explore the attraction between them, follow where

it might lead. But somehow he couldn't do that to Carly. Especially now. The Montavian press would eat her alive. Even his usually open-minded father would wonder if Carly had anything to do with his recent problems. As if she could.

"You know the expectations my country has of the kind of woman I should…date."

He'd almost said *marry,* but that was as ludicrous as this conversation. Carly didn't even know his true identity. She might not even be interested in the kind of frenetic lifestyle a royal lived.

"Their expectations never bothered you before. What happened to the devil-may-care prince I knew at Princeton?"

Luc pulled a hand down his face. "His brother died. And everything changed."

Carson pivoted to stare out the window. When he spoke again, his voice was low and thoughtful. "Sometimes a man is forced to do things he doesn't want to for the good of all concerned."

"I knew you would understand." Luc pushed up from the upholstered chair. "Thank you. I'll let you know when my travel arrangements are complete."

Carson spun back to him. His tone bordered on desperation. "We're having a dance Saturday night. You will stay until then? Take Carly for one last date?"

How unlike Carson to pry into another's personal life. But he supposed his old friend had his best interests at heart. And if truth be told, Luc desired a few more days in Carly's company, a few more days of her wit and wisdom to carry him through the times ahead.

"I had already set Monday for departure."

Tension eased from Carson's body. "Good. Good. That gives us three more days."

Luc extended his right hand. How hospitable of Carson to want more time in his company. "You are a fine friend, Carson. If ever I can repay your kindness—"

To his surprise, Carson reached in his desk and took out a set of car keys. "As a matter of fact, you can. Some tools and camping supplies were left behind the night of the fire. Take the Jeep." The rancher's lips quirked in a sheepish grin. "Take Carly, too. I promised her a look at Sky Bluff."

Luc couldn't hold back a chuckle. "If I didn't know you better, I'd say you were trying to play the matchmaker."

Grin turning to a scowl, Carson tossed him the keys. "Get lost, Jardine."

And as Luc closed the door behind him, he found himself wishing that he could do exactly that.

The open-air Jeep bounced over rocks and gullies on the trip to the far side of the vast ranch. With little more than cattle trails for roads the ride was invigorating, to say the least. Carly loved it.

The Oklahoma wind kicked up, hot and relentless, while in the west thunderheads gathered. Trailing streaks of red and orange, the late afternoon sun faded toward evening.

"Do you think it will rain before we get back?" Her hair whipped loose from its clamp and slapped her cheeks.

"Hard to tell." Luc looked glorious, all sexy and tumbled with his wild curls blowing back from his movie-star face.

"Maybe we should have put the top on this thing."

He followed her gaze to the thunderheads but didn't appear the least concerned. "Scared of getting wet?"

They both grinned, knowing better. "Actually I think it might be fun. When I was a kid, I loved walking in the rain."

"Nothing like an adventure to get the adrenaline pumping."

Her adrenaline was already pumping enough by being with him. Since that night in the pool their relationship had grown exponentially, become warmer, more comfortable and definitely more personal. They'd exchanged enough mind-numbing kisses that she had finally decided to stop fighting the inevitable and let it happen. She loved him, prince or pauper, cowboy or commoner. No man would ever fill her heart this way again.

But she was a realist, too, aware that this summer with Luc was an interlude soon to be over. Every minute spent in his company would be a memory to revisit when she returned to the real world. Or when he discovered her original motive for seeking out his company.

"That looks like the campsite up ahead." Luc gunned the engine, and the force thrust Carly back against the seat.

She laughed. "You drive like this is the autobahn."

"The autobahn is not half so much fun. Too predictable. This, on the other hand…"

He wheeled the Jeep to the right, slammed on the brakes and came to a stop. A cloud of dust engulfed them.

"Here we are safe and sound." He leaped from the driver's seat.

Carly waved the dust away, coughing. "That's open for interpretation."

A distant rumble of thunder had them both glancing toward the west.

"Better hurry. That cloud is coming faster than I thought."

"What exactly was it that Mr. Benedict wanted us to bring back from here?"

"Anything and everything we find. In our haste the night of the fire, some camping gear and supplies were left behind. None of the cowboys have had time to retrieve them."

Carly wandered over to the now-dead campfire where Luc had first kissed her.

"Look." She held up a half-empty bag of dried marshmallows. "Remember these?"

"Do I?" Tossing a dusty bedroll into the Jeep, he covered the distance between them. "You had marshmallow here." His index finger tapped her lips. "And I couldn't resist doing this."

He covered her mouth with his in a quick, hungry kiss. "Delicious," he said, eyes dancing with mischief.

A splat of rain plopped onto her tilted chin. Luc kissed it away, then winked. "We should hurry."

Bemused and blissful, Carly set about to load everything she could find into the Jeep. By the time they'd gathered all the salvageable items, the rain peppered down in earnest.

Luc fashioned a plastic tarp over the camping gear and jumped into the truck. Rummaging under a sleeping bag, he found his hat, plopped it on Carly's head, then cranked the engine and roared off.

The shower turned to a torrent.

"This rain is unbelievable. Is it always like this?" he shouted. Drenched hair was plastered to his head.

Grabbing Luc's hat as the wind threatened to tear it away, Carly returned the shout. "Typical Oklahoma cloudburst. Fast and heavy. Hopefully it will let up soon."

"I had planned to show you Sky Bluff."

Carly leaned forward and dumped a trough of rain from the hat brim. "What's stopping you? It's only a little water."

Luc grinned, his teeth white and even in a face shining with rain. "You are one unusual woman, Miss Carpenter." He turned the wheel in the opposite direction of the ranch. "Let's go for it."

They drove through the wind and rain, laughing each time the Jeep hit a hole and splattered mud on them. In seconds the dirt was washed away.

Soon water rushed over the earth in narrow rivers and the land became boggy and slick. Luc slowed the Jeep through a wooded incline.

The utility vehicle slipped sideways. Tires spun, then caught and chugged onward. Luc downshifted. "This path through the woods is perfect for horses, but—"

His lips formed a tight line as the Jeep slid again. Carly grabbed on to the seat with both hands. The muddy path suddenly bogged and the left side of the vehicle tilted downward…and stopped.

At the sudden cessation of motion, Carly rocked back and forth in the seat. "Uh-oh."

Luc got out to survey the situation. When he climbed back in, his expression was glum. "We're stuck."

"Figured as much."

The canopy of trees provided a measure of shelter, but they were both soaked to the skin. The rain, having done its work, eased to a shower.

Draping an arm over the steering wheel, Luc turned in the seat to face her. "Sorry. Are you upset?"

She blinked at him, dumbfounded. "Why would I be upset? This was my idea. Maybe you should be mad at me."

His jaw worked as if they were in some sort of serious trouble. "You are my responsibility, and I have brought you out here and gotten you stranded."

"Oh, please." She squeezed water from her dripping hair and tossed it over one shoulder. "Give it a rest. I'm an adult, accountable for myself. You aren't the king of the world, responsible for anyone and everyone. We're stuck, not stranded on a deserted island."

He gave her a strange look, and she could have bitten off her own tongue. Why had she said that?

"At least we have the cell phone to call for help." He withdrew the instrument from beneath the seat, took one look at it and began to laugh.

Carly laughed, too, though she had no idea why. At

least he was cheerful again instead of feeling so all-fired responsible. "What's so funny?"

"It's dead."

"Dead?"

"Yes. Dead. Kaput. Finis." He sliced a finger across his throat and shrugged. "No signal at all."

Carly laughed harder. Luc joined her.

When they finally regained their composure, Luc said, "Most women of my acquaintance would not find this situation amusing."

Carly didn't need to be reminded that she was nothing like the women in Luc's real life. "What should we do? Walk back to the ranch?"

"Too late. We would be walking in the dark before we had traveled halfway. This is rattlesnake country. I don't recommend night walks."

"Okay. Then what do you suggest? Make like Robinson Crusoe until morning?"

"Do you have a better idea?"

"No." The idea of spending a night in the woods with Luc was scary and alluring. Just the two of them, alone.

"The plastic tarp will make an adequate shelter." The humor returned to his face. "And we have marshmallows for sustenance."

"What more could we wish for?" Her accepting reaction surprised her. Where was the city girl who only days ago had been reluctant to go on a camping trip?

They set to work, pulling supplies from those they had salvaged at the campsite. Luc rigged the plastic tarp between trees, fastening the sides down with vines so that it created a tentlike structure. Using his bare hands, he swept away the layer of wet leaves to reveal a barely damp floor.

Several times Carly wanted to tell him that he was pretty handy for a prince. Of course, she couldn't. He'd be livid to know of her deceit. And tonight her job, the count and Luc's kingdom were far away.

She ducked under the tarp, where Luc, on haunches, put the finishing touches on the cozy shelter.

"I don't suppose you found any extra clothes in that backpack, did you?" Her jeans and shirt weighed a ton and stuck to her skin.

He unzipped the bag and rummaged inside, coming out with a camouflage jacket and pants. "Someone must have planned a hunt."

"Lucky for us." She knelt beside him. "Anything else in there?"

"A plastic poncho, a box of Band-Aids, an energy bar and—" His lips quirked as he hoisted a tiny bra.

She resisted a glance at her ample chest. "Uh, no. I don't think so. But if the rain poncho is long enough I could change into that and you can have the camo."

"Much as I would enjoy seeing you in this—" He held up the clear plastic garment.

Carly fought off a blush. "Scratch that idea. We can share the camo and use the poncho for cover."

"You take the camo. You're soaked."

"No way. You take it." The man was a future king. She couldn't let him remain in wet clothing all night. He might get sick.

He held up a hand for silence. "A compromise. You wear the jacket. I will take the pants."

Without waiting for further argument, Luc tossed the jacket onto her lap and stepped outside. "Call me when you have changed."

Carly stripped down to her panties, decided to leave those, damp or not, and then shrugged into the jacket. She watched Luc's broad back soak up more rain as she buttoned the garment. The tapered tails struck her at midthigh—much less revealing than her bikini but somehow more uncomfortably suggestive.

"Okay. I'm decent. Sort of."

Luc ducked back under the tarp with a chuckle. "I'll be the judge of that." He took one look at her and froze. "Your legs are most amazing."

Holding to the tails as if a capricious wind would lift them, she rolled her eyes and shrugged. "The most amazing thing about my legs right now is that they're covered in goose bumps. Now stop staring and get out of those wet clothes before, as my mama always says, you catch your death. I'll turn my back." She did.

In the tiny space, charged with the knowledge that they were both basically naked, Carly jumped at the sound of his zipper. Her breathing accelerated.

Sheesh. It was a zipper, not a machete.

He cleared his throat. Was he as aware of her as she was of him?

"All done."

She turned. Whoever owned the camo was a few inches shorter and far outweighed the prince. The pants struck Luc just above the ankle. He held the front together in one hand.

The silly sight broke the tension. Carly giggled. "Looks like you need a belt—and a ruffle."

"I would settle for a piece of rope."

She gazed around. "Hmm. No rope, but here's a thought—cut one of the straps off the backpack and use it to tie the front loops together."

"Beauty and resourcefulness. What more could a man ask?"

He was good at that, throwing little compliments around to make her feel special. Did he do the same for all his women?

While he followed her suggestion, fashioning a makeshift belt, Carly took the single blanket and draped it over his shoulders, resisting the urge to caress the bare, muscled skin.

They were alone and barely covered. Better not start something she wasn't ready to finish.

On his knees, Luc gazed up and smiled his thanks. Carly's heart stutter-stepped. She longed to blurt out the truth, to tell him she loved him and go with whatever happened. Instead, she dropped a kiss at the corner of his mouth and turned to look outside.

The rain had slowed to a drip after washing the woods clean and fresh. Along with a chorus of invisible tree frogs, birds had once more ventured out to serenade them. The forest appeared mystical, enchanted even.

Luc moved to her side. "Care to share my blanket?"

Without awaiting her reply, he wrapped the scratchy wool around them both and pulled her close. The warm dampness of his skin blended with the remnants of his cologne. Carly breathed him in, knowing his uniquely masculine scent would linger in her memory for a long time to come.

"Look," he murmured. His warm breath brushed her ear, made her shiver. "A rainbow."

The most vivid colors, blues and reds, yellows and greens, arched above the trees. "Gorgeous," she murmured.

"Uh-huh." He nuzzled her neck. "You are indeed."

Carly almost believed she was. Luc made her feel desirable, womanly. And she hadn't done one bumbling thing in days.

"The rainbow, silly. It's beautiful."

"Oh, that." He squinted upward. "Want to follow it? Find the pot of gold at the end?"

Smiling, Carly shook her head. All the gold in the world couldn't buy what she felt for Luc or what she wanted from him. "I never really cared about money that much."

"No? Then what is it you would like to have?"

You. Forever. But she couldn't say that.

Instead she lifted her face and kissed him.

"Ah," he said with a twinkle. "I can gladly accommodate."

And he did, kissing her until her heart sang and her blood hummed. Then they sat together beneath the blanket, arms around waists, while the rainbow dissipated and the sun slipped beyond the horizon.

"As a boy," Luc said after a while, "I enjoyed camping in the wilderness this way."

"With your family?" Somehow Carly had never

imagined royals as rugged outdoorsmen, but Luc challenged all her preconceptions.

"Mostly with Philippe and our…servants."

She knew he meant bodyguards and yearned for him to share the whole truth about his life. "You and your brother were so close. Losing him must have nearly killed you."

"There are those who wish it had."

"Luc! What an awful thing to say."

His chest rose and fell. He looked at her, then quickly glanced away, training his eyes on the wet, sleepy woods. "May I tell you something? Something I've never shared with anyone?"

Carly's pulse ratcheted up a notch. Did he finally trust her enough to reveal his identity? "You can tell me anything."

He sighed and snuggled her closer, resting his chin on her head. "I know that. And I am grateful."

He didn't speak for several heavy moments while Carly waited, barely breathing. If he revealed his identity, would it mean he cared for her? Was trusting the same as loving?

"The day my brother died—" He stopped, sucked in a ragged breath.

Carly laid a comforting hand on his bare chest. Luc's need to share his worst heartache was much more important than her neurotic need for affirmation.

"What happened?"

"We were skiing. On holiday, you see. Having such fun together. Philippe had upended a Thermos of chocolate on my new ski jacket. Pure accident, of course. But then he skied off, laughing at my indignation, and I gave chase." A ghost of a smile trembled around his supple mouth. "We were so competitive." He shook his head. "No. Not we. Me. I was the competitor, always pushing."

Suddenly Carly knew. "You blame yourself for what happened."

As if he didn't hear, Luc continued. "We raced down the mountain at breakneck speed on an uncharted trail. Philippe was ahead. For once in his life, he was winning." Luc squeezed his eyes shut, his voice rough and deep.

"Even now I see the flash of his red skis against the powdery snow, hear his triumphant laugh...right before he disappeared into the silence."

"Oh, Luc." Carly tightened her hold on his waist and laid her cheek against his chest, aching for him. Beneath her ear, his heart pounded.

"The ledge was hidden by the snow. A white abyss. I rushed down to him, fractured my ankle in the process—but what did that matter? He was gone, broken and twisted on the rocks."

"How did you ever get help? Did rescuers come looking for you?"

He frowned as though the question was foolish. "I skied down the mountain."

"On a broken ankle?"

"My brother was dead, Carly." His tone had shifted to quiet resignation, an acceptance of what he could not change.

She studied his beloved face, saw the tragedy hidden behind the blue eyes. "It wasn't your fault."

"I should never have raced him that way. Philippe was not the skier I am. All our lives I had defended him against those who took advantage of his gentle nature. But in the end, I was no different than them."

Funny that Luc didn't realize the obvious—that he had always been the strong one, the true leader.

"You protected him, stood up for him and most of all loved him. His death was a tragic, unavoidable accident."

He gave her a small smile that never reached his eyes. "Rumors flew for a while that I had somehow arranged Philippe's accident to steal his birthright."

Carly gasped at the ugly allegation. "How terrible. And how untrue."

"Yes, but I can't alter public opinion."

"Someday people will know you well enough to realize the truth. They will see your heart, as I do, and they'll know."

He placed a finger beneath her chin and tilted it up. "You are good for me, Carly."

And then he kissed her. The warm, sweet gratitude of his kiss nearly broke her heart. She loved him so much. How could any idiot on the planet not see his worth?

Gradually his kisses changed, became far more than gratitude. He kissed her until her eyes crossed and her blood heated. Some female part of her brain recognized that he wanted her. Maybe he didn't love her as she did him, but he felt something.

When he laid them back against the padded cotton

sleeping bag, she didn't resist. If tonight was all she could have, she would take it.

"Luc," she whispered.

"Hmm?"

Night sounds pulsed around them. In the dim moonlight she watched his beloved face study her. She stroked his jaw, dipped a finger in that near dimple next to his mouth and found the courage to say, "There's something I have to tell you before—"

His thumb, which had been rubbing sensuous circles on her collarbone, stilled. "And that would be?"

She swallowed, pulse clattering against her temples. "I love you."

"I know, *chérie*," he whispered, accent stronger than usual. "I know. And it makes me both delighted and despairing."

She hadn't expected a jubilant reception, but sadness? "Why?"

"My life is complicated, Carly. Much more than I can explain." He stroked the side of her face one time before sliding down beside her to lie on his back and stare up at the blue plastic roof. "I would never want to hurt you."

From anyone else, the words would sound like a kiss-off. But she knew Luc's dilemma, understood now more than ever the load of responsibility and obligation weighing on him. She knew she didn't fit in his world and never would.

"I'm a big girl. You won't hurt me." Yes, he would. But she would live. Maybe.

"Now *I* must again tell *you* something, though I

cannot tell you all that I wish." His voice was rough, unsteady.

More revelation? More worries about his future as king?

She rolled toward him, tried to read his expression in the semidarkness. "Okay."

He hesitated long enough that she knew the news was not good. Her heart tumbled to her chilled toes.

"I will be leaving soon. Much sooner than I had planned."

Carly closed her eyes against the sudden stab of pain. So this is how it would end. One night or none. She had to decide.

"Is something wrong?" She tried to understand. Wanted to believe that what called him away was important enough for him to leave her.

"Yes." The bedroll rustled as he propped up on his elbow to look at her. In the dim light his blue eyes were serious, pleading for her to understand.

Carly touched his arm and said softly, "Tell me. You know you can."

He drew in a deep breath and exhaled in a gusty whoosh. "My family's business is of a sensitive nature. Everyone, especially the leadership, must be completely aboveboard in every respect. Otherwise our work is jeopardized. I already have Philippe's death as a mark against me."

Even after sharing his deepest hurt, he still talked in circles, couching his identity in terms of business. Little pinpricks of disappointment poked at Carly.

"I'm not sure I follow."

"There appears to be a movement afoot to have me declared unsuitable for leadership."

Carly bolted upright. "But how? Why? You've done nothing wrong. I can vouch for that."

He pressed her back down, stroked her hair as if she was the one in distress. "Someone in my country— a competitor perhaps—has started rumors that I left Montavia because I am out of control and not worthy of the—" he stopped himself.

Carly knew he'd almost said *the throne*.

"Worthy of taking over for your father?" she finished.

"Exactly."

"But I don't understand. How can a few unsubstantiated allegations be taken seriously."

"They aren't few. And they aren't unsubstantiated. My father e-mailed a number of photographs that are being circulated in the tabloids. They show me in compromising situations. With half-dressed women. Drunk. High. Carousing."

"But that's crazy. How could anyone get such pictures of you when you aren't even there?"

"They appear to be current, but somehow they must have been altered to give the appearance of misdeed on my part."

"Current? How is that possible?"

As soon as she spoke, the knowledge hit her like a pie in the face. All her inward warnings suddenly clicked into focus. Hadn't she seen the red flags, the signs of something not quite right with Count Broussard's claim that he was only concerned for the prince's welfare?

Horror seeped into her.

Was she responsible? Had the pictures come from her? And Count Broussard?

"Ohmigosh."

Her mind raced with the damage her actions could have caused. Had she been a dupe, used by Luc's advisor to supply the very information that, when tweaked, could present the prince in a less-than-flattering light?

"Oh, Luc, I'm so sorry." She took his face between her palms. She had to investigate and, if she was involved, find a way to stop Count Broussard. No one had a right to keep Luc from the throne. "You are going to be a great CEO for your father's company. Don't you dare let some sniveling, jealous guy like—" She bit her lip and tried again. "Don't you dare let someone rob your company of the best leader they will ever have."

He drew her against his warm, muscled chest and kissed her temple. "Anyone who plays such devious games must be stopped. It is my duty and my right to safeguard my company's future. Thank you for making me realize that, for showing me so many truths I had never understood before. I will be forever grateful."

No. No, he wouldn't. But she couldn't tell him that. She could only thrill in the knowledge that somehow she'd helped this future king recognize his destiny. He was an incredible man, strong and brave and true. Far more man than she could ever have.

For soon enough Luc would discover that it was she who had betrayed him. Soon he would view her words of love as lies told to trap him, and the man she loved would hate her.

Heart breaking, Carly pulled away. With trembling lips she said, "We should get some sleep."

And then she lay down and, with back turned, pressed her face into the slick nylon bedding and let the silent tears fall.

Luc lay in the darkness for a long time, listening to Carly's soft breathing. Not one but two startling revelations had come to him tonight when he'd held her and listened to her sweet words of love and encouragement.

He would never be Father or Philippe, but he loved his country and would work hard to make it strong and prosperous. He would honor his brother's memory by becoming a good and able king. Carly had opened his eyes to that, just as she had helped him accept that Philippe's death had not been his fault. Intellectually he had always known. Tonight his heart believed.

All because of the wise and wonderful woman beside him.

With all his soul he wanted to tell her everything, just as he longed to take her home to his family.

He wanted to. But he couldn't.

Introducing Carly into his world would hurt her more than leaving her behind. For all her strength, she was a sensitive woman. What would the press and the snobbish society of his peers do to her?

His country was deeply traditional. They simply assumed that when his wild oats were sown, their prince would make an appropriate match with a Montavian woman of suitable lineage and produce an heir.

No, he couldn't subject Carly to the kind of painful scrutiny and cruelty that the press was capable of.

Worse yet, how would she react to the knowledge that she had come to know him under pretense? That he was not who he pretended to be?

He tossed and turned in the tiny, damp shelter, finally coming to a wrenching decision.

He'd been selfish long enough, both to Carly and to his country. He would return home—alone—to his duties as the future king of Montavia.

Chapter Ten

Carly was mad.

By the time she arrived back in her guest room the next morning, she was a woman on a mission.

Last night had been both wonderful and terrible. She'd loved the time with Luc and had wanted to stay in their magical hideaway forever. But with the morning came reality. The cell phone had acquired a signal in the clear, cloudless morning, and before she and Luc had reloaded the Jeep, a surprisingly chipper Carson Benedict had arrived to escort them back to the ranch.

Carly slammed the heel of her fist against her laptop. Following a brief Internet search, she accepted her culpability. Count Broussard had indeed used her. She didn't know why, but the information leaking all over the Montavian media could only have come from one place—her.

How could she have been so stupid?

Desperate for a shower and breakfast, Carly refused to pamper herself with either. Too much damage had been done by her carelessness, and she had to make up for lost time.

If it was the last investigation she ever did, she would nail that count's head to the wall. A royal advisor who would double-cross his own prince was likely to be dirty in other areas, too. And she planned to uncover every wicked thing he'd ever done and share them with the world. She couldn't undo her mistakes, but she could stop the villain from hurting Luc any more. By handling things very delicately, she might also put an end to the ugly speculation that was damaging Luc's reputation.

She grabbed the telephone and asked for an overseas operator. In minutes she had resigned her job with Broussard, saying Luc had left the ranch and she didn't know where he had gone. The count was upset and urged her to track the prince down again, but Carly refused. She wanted nothing more to do with the evil man who wanted to hurt the man she loved.

Immensely relieved to no longer be in the employ of Luc's enemy, she rifled through two weeks' worth of documentation and photos and slid the appropriate pieces into a manila envelope for over-nighting. King Alexandre needed to see the originals, as well as her day-to-day reports of Luc's activities before he would accept the truth.

Praying that her plan would work, she made several more phone calls, trying not to fret about the charges to her credit card now that she was, yet again, unemployed.

When Luc knocked on her door late that afternoon, Carly was putting the final touches on her plan. At the sound of his voice, she tossed a housecoat over her work and opened the door.

Twinkling blue eyes took in her appearance. In her haste to do damage control in Montavia, she hadn't bothered to change clothes. Her feet and legs remained bare. Her hair felt as if she'd just crawled out of bed. And she still wore the camouflage jacket.

"I could grow deeply fond of that particular fashion statement."

She must look like roadkill. Luc, on the other hand, appeared fresh and rested. He had changed into slacks and a casual button-up shirt that matched his eyes. Even his naturally messy hair seemed tamer and more refined.

She glanced down at her bare toes and shrugged. "What can I say? I'm a regular trendsetter."

Luc's warm chuckle wrapped around her like a caress. "I have come to walk with you to the dining room."

Everything in her wanted to go, to squeeze in every second with her charming prince. But even though she hadn't eaten a bite all day, she couldn't. Not now. She couldn't be with him again until she'd done everything possible to repair the damage she'd unwittingly done to him.

"I think I'll skip dinner tonight, if you don't mind. I'm pretty tired."

"I will bring something to you instead. We could eat here, in your room."

She shook her head. Why didn't he just leave before she fell at his feet and confessed everything? She needed time. Time to make things right again.

"I'd rather not."

Disappointment flitted across his face. "Is something wrong?"

"You're leaving soon, Luc," she said gently. "I'd better start getting used to not having you around so much."

That much was true, though it was far short of the real reasons for her refusal.

He touched her face, and the feel of his skin against hers melted her insides. "You are a very special lady."

Special. Yeah, well, special didn't quite cut it for a woman who'd fallen head over heels in love with the wrong man. "Don't worry. I'm okay." Sad maybe, and madder than a wet cat, but okay. "Don't give me another thought."

And if you will please go away, I'll try to fix the mess I've gotten you into. She started to close the door. "If you'll excuse me—"

Luc stopped the door with an outstretched palm. "There is a dance tomorrow night. You will be there?"

To erase the worry from his expression, she smiled and said in a falsely chipper voice, "Sure. Wouldn't miss it."

At that moment she would agree to anything to get him out of her room. She was about to crumble, to cling and cry. And she still had to make a trip into town and keep a date with the FedEx man…and King Alexandre of Montavia.

* * *

Saturday afternoon, Carly, wearing a ratty old terry robe and a blue-green beauty mask that felt like Elmer's glue, tried to relax in a chair while Tina Osborne sat cross-legged on the floor and painted her toenails.

"I don't know what possessed me to let you do this," she said to the teen.

Tina, in lounge pajamas with Bite Me across the behind, said, "Your fingernails are next. And then we'll pluck your eyebrows."

Carly shrank backward. "You will not!"

"Hold still. I just painted the sole of your foot Passionate Cherry."

Ever since Luc had insisted she attend tonight's dance, Carly had been a basket case. She hadn't intended to see him again until she had found a way to discredit Count Broussard and make amends for the bad press reports. But he was leaving Monday, and after Teddi Benedict arrived at her doorstep with a fabulous after-five dress, Carly had been overcome with the most unstoppable desire to make Luc very sorry he was going to walk away and leave her. She was good for him. Well, okay. So, she'd done a couple of sneaky things. But when all of this started, she hadn't expected to fall in love with him! Couldn't he see that?

"I still think it's weird that the Benedicts thought they owed me that outfit simply because of a few mishaps beyond their control." Teddi had claimed the dress came as recompense for all the trouble Carly had experienced at the ranch.

"Hey, don't complain. I wish she'd brought me a hot

little number like that. I could knock Dirk's eyes out across the room."

"You will anyway."

Tina giggled. "Probably. He's hopelessly in love with me."

Carly envied Tina's confidence.

She motioned toward her rigid face. "When can I wash this gunk off—"

The telephone interrupted her.

Tina straightened and pointed the polish applicator toward her. "Don't move. I'll hand the phone to you."

With cotton jammed between her toes and green slime on her face, Carly wouldn't dream of moving. Lips stiff, she took the phone and muttered into it. "Hullo."

"Carly."

Her pulse stuttered to a standstill.

"Eric?" Oh, no.

"I've had some very strange calls the last couple of days. It's taken me some time to figure out what's going on, but now everything has become clear. For some asinine reason that I don't care to hear, you've been misrepresenting my agency as your own."

No pleasant exchange of greetings. Just slam me against the wall and cuff me.

"Will you let me explain?" Carly asked quietly, eyes shifting to Tina, who pretended not to listen.

"Explain? I am a detective." Recognizing the controlled rage in his tone, Carly knew she was in deep doo-doo. "I don't require explanations. Especially when a very high-ranking official in the Montavian government is threatening lawsuit because of your incompetence."

She tried to interrupt, to tell him that Broussard was angry because she refused to do his dirty work, but Eric was on a roll.

"If you weren't my sister-in-law, I'd have you arrested. Instead it gives me great pleasure to simply say, you're fired. Even Meg can't save your butt this time. You're done, Carly. For good. You were never cut out to be a private investigator."

Carly's palms grew moist and her insides trembled, but her words came out with surprising calm. "You know what, Eric? I don't care. Broussard is a traitor, trying to discredit his own leader. By ending the investigation, I stopped him cold. And if that means losing my job, then I can live with that. But I couldn't live with hurting someone I care about. Can you?"

"Fired, Carly. That's what I care about."

Before she could utter another word of defense, the line went dead. Carly contemplated the silent receiver and her questionable future for several long seconds before handing the phone to Tina.

The teen capped the nail polish. "From the look on your face, I'd say that didn't go well."

Carly studied her Passionate Cherry toenails. They looked good. Other than the humiliation of being fired and the sweat on her palms, she felt pretty good, too. Now how stupid was that? Her dream career was forever gone, her sister probably hated her and yet Carly felt wonderfully free.

Though the money would have been great and the opportunity to prove herself as a good investigator had been within her grasp, doing the right thing for Luc mattered more. She'd screwed things up at first, but if her idea worked, Broussard would never hurt Luc again. And that was far more important than any job would ever be.

Feeling the oddest sense of relief, she swiped a hand over her robe and offered her fingertips to Tina. "Proceed, please." A tiny grin tried to crack the mud mask. "Then bring on the tweezers."

Luc stood in front of the mirror, his gut in a bigger knot than his silk tie. Tonight was the last night he planned to spend with Carly, and he was as anxious as a school boy on his first date. She had avoided him all day, and though he understood her true reasons, he missed her terribly. Missed her zany laugh, her warmth, her honesty. And he missed holding her, kissing her.

He slapped his collar down and glared at his reflection. "What a mess."

His public life was in shambles and all he could think about was Carly.

How did a man say goodbye to a woman who had done so much for him? Who had made him realize how much he loved his country and wanted to be its leader. Who had helped him finally believe that he was not responsible for his brother's accident.

And—if he was honest enough to admit it—had captured his heart with her goodness.

A woman like that deserved so much more than a farewell dance.

For the thousandth time in three days, the idea of

inviting her to Montavia intruded. Not now but later, when the scandal rags had been silenced and his critics along with them.

Would she go if he asked her? Or would she be angry that he had hidden his identity from her?

Since Philippe's death he had kept his worries to himself, but tonight he longed to talk to his father and seek his wise counsel. Before he could change his mind, he grabbed the telephone.

The private family line rang only once before his father barked into the receiver.

"Luc. I was about to phone you."

Something in the king's clipped Montavian French warned him. Luc tensed. "Have more problems arisen?"

"The same problems have become much clearer and much more disturbing. Son, I must insist you come home at once. Without delay."

"I am booked to fly out on Monday."

"No. From what we have learned, you need to be here with us, where we can assist you. My jet is en route as we speak."

"This is not making sense to me."

A long, weary sigh winged across the miles. "Arturo was so concerned about your well-being that he hired a private investigator to find out the truth. As difficult as it is for me to accept, I fear the photos and dossier reveal the trouble you are in."

Luc collapsed onto a chair. An investigator? Here? But who?

"I assure you, sir, I am not in any trouble, but some-

one in Montavia is going to be when I get to the bottom
of this." Anger began to replace the shock. "Tell me,
exactly what kind of trouble am I supposedly in?"

"Addicted and debauched, the reports say, with a
recommendation for institutional care at once. There is
an excellent facility outside of Zurich."

Institutional care? How had things gotten so dis-
torted? "Those reports are a total fabrication."

"I want to believe you, my son, but how and why
would a private investigator fabricate an official report
such as this?"

"I don't know. But I plan to find out. Do you have
the name of the investigator? He and I need to have a
serious talk."

Luc heard a rustle of papers. "Here it is. An agency
out of Dallas, Texas. Wright Stuff Investigations. And
the detective's name is…Carly Carpenter."

Carly knew something was wrong the minute Luc
entered the ballroom. From her spot next to Teddi
Benedict, who had gushed compliments about Carly's
elegant black dress and carefully applied makeup, she
observed his stiff gait, his curt nod to other guests.

Even upset, he was so very handsome in his dark
suit and blue shirt, his curly hair as untamed as his expression.

He searched the room, found her and strode through
the crowd of cowboys and ladies in their Saturday best.
A waiter approached, offered a drink, but Luc shook
his head, never taking his cold stare off Carly's face—
a stare that said he *knew.*

She wanted to turn and run. Instead she stood her ground, heart thudding painfully. Might as well face the music and get it over with.

"Dance with me," he commanded, tone as glacial as his eyes.

Her stomach jittered as he took her into his arms and spun her out onto the floor. Where his body had welcomed hers before, he now held her as he had the newspaper on the day they'd met—as though he loathed her touch.

His beloved mouth, usually so mobile and eager to laugh, formed a hard slash. His jaw flexed repeatedly.

"Is something wrong?"

"I think you can answer that better than I."

Yes, he knew. And he hated her.

"I'm sorry," she whispered. "I wanted to tell you everything, but first—"

"But first what, Carly? First you wanted to collect your fee? First you wanted to destroy my reputation completely? Even my own father has begun to believe your lies."

"My reports were the absolute truth. Count Broussard was the one—"

He jerked her tightly against him. "How far would you have taken your charade? Would you have snapped pictures of us making love and sold them to the highest bidder?"

Mortified at his suggestion, she tried to pull away. Though she was no fragile female, he held fast, twirling smoothly around the dance floor as though nothing were amiss.

"I took the job before I knew you. Before I fell in love with you." She choked on the threatening tears, desperate for him to understand.

For a scant second his demeanor softened, and behind the cold glare Carly saw the awful hurt.

"Carly," he said, fingers coming up to touch her cheek. But then he caught himself, dropped his hand and stepped back. He executed a stiff, formal bow, then turned and walked away.

What was left of her heart shattered. Everything in her wanted to streak across the room, fall to her knees and beg for forgiveness.

But what purpose would that serve? She'd known all along that he was out of her league. A prince. A future king. Even if she had not betrayed him so completely, he would still have left her.

Her face burned. Her head ached with unshed tears.

For one shining moment klutzy Carly had felt beautiful. But the clock had struck midnight and the fairy tale was over.

Luc gripped the veranda railing and drew in long, steadying draughts of warm night air. His insides trembled. He hadn't hurt this badly since Philippe's funeral. He should have been bitter and angry, but instead he ached with the knowledge that the woman he'd come to love—he stifled a groan. Damn it, he loved her.

Footsteps warned him of someone's approach. He didn't bother to look up when Carson appeared at his side.

"Everything okay?"

Luc gave a short, mirthless laugh. "Nothing is okay."

A lively two-step wafted out from behind him. He wondered if one of the cowboys had asked Carly to dance. She'd looked so beautiful. He'd wanted to drink in the sight of her as a memory to revisit in the days ahead. And the way she'd felt in his arms—all woman, soft and feminine. Her sweet scent still lingered on his jacket.

"Care to talk about it?"

The red light of a passing jet winked in the Oklahoma sky. He watched it blend with the stunning display of the Milky Way, remembering Carly's complaint that she couldn't see stars in the city. She would have loved the Montavian sky.

"The palace plane is en route, along with a host of special agents. I'll be gone by morning."

"Is that what you were telling Carly?"

"No."

"Then why was she crying?"

Luc tilted his head, frowning into the darkness. "Crying? Are you certain?"

"I hate when women cry. What did you do? Break her heart?"

"She broke mine." And then because he knew this was one person he could trust, Luc told Carson everything.

"Let me get this straight," Carson said when he'd finished. "Carly didn't bother to tell you that she's a private eye? And you, in turn, didn't bother to tell her your real identity."

"She already knew."

"That's not the point. You were no more honest with her than she was with you."

"My reasons were more valid." But were they? Long after he had grown to trust her, to rely upon her and, yes, to love her, he had kept the secret. There was nothing fair in that.

Over the lively music inside the house Luc heard the drone of a car engine. Headlights swung off the gravel road and came down the driveway.

"Looks like we have more company." Carson's growl indicated his general dislike of running a guest ranch.

A late-model sports car pulled within a few yards of the veranda, the lights sweeping across Carson and Luc. The driver killed the motor and shoved the door open.

A tall, leggy blonde leaped out of the car and strode toward them. She was classy, elegant, gorgeous—and she knew it.

"I'm looking for my sister, Carly Carpenter."

"Marvelous Meg." Luc believed he'd only thought the name until Meg shot him a look.

"You must know my sister."

"Indeed."

She stuck out a long, manicured hand. "I'm Meg Wright. Can you tell me where to find Carly?"

"Wright?" Luc stiffened. "As in Wright Stuff Investigations? The agency Carly works for?" The company that had caused him so much grief.

"*Did* work for until this afternoon. That's why I'm here. To be sure she's okay."

"Did work for? What do you mean?"

The beautiful Meg eyed him coolly. "I'm afraid I don't know you, sir. So if you will direct me to my sister...."

Luc stepped in front of her, blocking her ascent onto the porch. "This gentleman is Carson Benedict, owner of the ranch. And I am Luc Gardner, a friend of Carly's."

Meg's glare would have frozen the Sahara. "Well. The incognito prince. So you are the one who has caused so many problems for my baby sister."

"On the contrary. Your sister has caused a scandal in my country and a great deal of difficulty for me personally."

"Let me tell you something, Mr. Prince." She pointed a hot-pink fingernail at his nose. "It took me a while to figure out what she's been up to, but I'm a good detective myself. Carly discovered that some guy in your government named Broussard has been altering reports and photographs, then feeding them to the media to make you look bad. When she refused to work for him, he pitched a fit and got her fired from my husband's agency."

Luc reeled backward, stunned. Could this be true? Could Arturo be the real culprit? "Carly lost her job?"

"Yes. For trying to protect you. For trying to do what was right. She's been busting her tail to discover why your royal advisor is out to get you. And all of the expenses have come out of her own pocket. Your fancy count promised a lot but has never paid her a dime."

Suddenly everything made sense. Arturo's constant

attempts to undermine Luc's confidence and his decisions. His fury when Luc disappeared, away from his influence. And the more recent insistence that the crown prince needed institutional care. He didn't know why his royal advisor hated him, but he planned to find out.

"Oh, Carly." She had been as much Arturo's victim as he had.

Carson's strong rancher's hand clapped him on the shoulder. "Maybe you should go talk to her. Get all this out in the open before you leave."

"I absolutely must." Sweet, sweet Carly. She'd done all that not for money but for him. "Do you mind if I talk to her first?" he said to Meg. "I will tell her you are here."

Meg studied him as if he were an insect in biology class. "My poor little sister is in love with you, isn't she?"

The words were music in his soul. "I hope so."

Meg favored him with a speculative half smile. "All right then, Mr. Prince. I'll give you fifteen minutes. Better make it count."

The security light barely penetrated the dark garden bench behind the house where Carly had collapsed in a heap of tears. Somewhere in the flight from the ballroom she'd lost one of her pretty high heels and now wore only one shoe. Not that it mattered. A woman like her had no business wasting good money on shoes. She couldn't buy sex appeal.

She swiped an arm across her sodden face and came

away with the last vestiges of her eye makeup. One more tear and her sinuses would swell closed and asphyxiate her.

All of this was her own fault. She'd known better than to fall in love with a prince.

"Carly."

Now she was hallucinating.

"Carly. *Mi amore.*"

That got her attention. "Luc?"

She sniffed and sat up, bewildered. What was he doing here?

Settling on the bench, he pulled her hand into his. His voice was quiet, pensive.

"I owe you an apology."

"No." She shook her head. The carefully upswept hairdo now tumbled around her face. "I misled you."

"True. But didn't I do the same?"

"You had a better reason. Any prince who goes around announcing his title has no chance of a private vacation retreat. But I never meant to harm you with my investigation." With her heart in her throat, she beseeched him. "Truly I didn't."

He shifted on the bench, turning to face her. "Your sister has arrived."

"Meg? Here? Oh, man. She's going to kill me."

"On the contrary. She will kill me if I don't do this correctly." A tiny smile lifted the corner of his beloved mouth. "She told me what you'd done, that you have sacrificed your career because of me."

"Count Broussard is trying to discredit you, Luc. I have to know why. And even if I never work again as a private investigator, I will stop him. You are your country's future. They need you."

"I know that. Because of you. And you can rest assured, with your help my name will be cleared, and when my father is ready to retire I *will* become king."

"With my help? You mean you'll let me work for you?" Being his employee would be agony, but she was willing to do anything to make amends.

"No, Carly. I will not allow you to work for me. Ever."

Her heart plummeted. The dratted tears threatened to clog up her sinuses again. "Then let me recommend my brother-in-law. He's an excellent—"

Luc laid a finger on her lips. "Shh. Let's talk no more of work, of blame and fault. No more of my royal advisor or the kingdom of Montavia." A pair of oceanic eyes studied her with an emotion that set her foolish heart hoping. "Carly, my love. I have been a self-absorbed man. And tonight I came very close to making the worst mistake of my life."

Carly's pulse rate rocketed into overdrive. She saw it in his eyes, heard it in his voice. But it was impossible.

With exquisite tenderness he lifted her hand and kissed her knuckles one by one. The beauty of his action brought new tears—tears of happiness.

"I almost walked away from the most incredible woman I've ever met. I love you, Carly. I want you to come home with me, to Montavia, to be my queen."

"Whoa, wait." She pulled away, suddenly terrified. Her heart hammered in trepidation as she stared into

the black Oklahoma night. "Me? A queen? Uh-uh.
Queen of Klutz maybe, but that's it."

"You don't love me, then? That, too, was a lie?"

She swung back to face him. "No! I love you with
all my heart. That's why I can't be your queen. Your
country would never accept someone like me."

"Like you?" With a scowl he drew her into his arms.
And, oh, his masculine chest was a wonderful place to
rest her aching head. "Then they would be fools and I
would not want to be their leader. For you are beautiful and wise, smart and witty. And full of kindness and
grace. Everything about you charms me. Everything."

She snuffled against his shirt. His woodsy cologne
must be going to her head, because she was starting to
believe him. "Even when I trip over your feet?"

"Even more so then. You delight me, fill me. Tonight when I walked out of that dance, I realized that
I am only half of myself without you. A man, especially a king, needs a strong woman beside him. That
woman is you, Carly. I can't do it without you. Please
come home with me."

She tilted her head to look at his beloved face, hoping, hoping, hoping. "But what will your family think?"

"My family and my country are important, but they
must accept me for who I am. I am not compliant, ever-
agreeable Philippe. I am not my traditional father. The
people of Montavia are wise. They will love you as I do."

Suddenly Carly saw herself through Luc's eyes.
She'd changed so much these past weeks. Loving Luc
and feeling his love for her filled her with a confidence
she'd never had before. She'd never be Marvelous Meg,

but that didn't matter anymore. She was the woman Luc loved. And that's all she needed.

Radiant joy shot through her.

"Will you just shut up then and kiss me? I'm real tired of talking."

Luc's laughter filled the night. "Not until you say yes."

Smiling, she grabbed his face between her hands and, lips barely brushing his, whispered, "Yes, yes, yes."

And then he crushed her to him. Her smile dissolved into the velvet warmth of his mouth and the promise of joy to come. He kissed her lips, her cheeks, her eyes, murmuring a delicious mix of French and English.

Much later he rested his forehead on hers, still holding her close. Her pulsing blood matched the pulsing of the night songs around them. In the distance the band played as a vocalist crooned, "Could I have this dance for the rest of my life?"

Luc cocked his head, listening. "I believe they are playing our song. Shall we?"

Dancing was a great excuse to stay in his arms a while longer, but she had a problem. She held out her bare toes. "I can't. I lost my shoe."

The grin she'd come to love so much tilted his lips.

"Did it look like this?" He reached behind him on the bench and brought out a silver-sequined sling.

"Where did you find…?"

To her delight, Carly's Prince Charming went down on one knee, lifted her foot in his strong hand and slid the heel into place.

Then he stood and executed a genteel bow. "May I?"

With her heart overflowing, Luc swept her into his arms and lovingly waltzed her beneath a golden Oklahoma moon.

She knew then that she would become Queen Carly, standing strong at the side of her man.

And she danced with the grace of a willow.

Epilogue

Carson Benedict gazed around at the palatial hall where a wedding reception for His Royal Highness Crown Prince Lucian Marcus Alexandre Jardine and his stunning bride, Princess Carly, was in full swing. Only years of friendship could have gotten Carson on an airplane and into this monkey suit. That, and the fact that he'd had a hand in getting the prince and his princess together in the first place.

Beside him his sister Teddi bounced and glowed in a lime-green formal. "Aren't they perfect together? Who would ever have thought Carly could look so regal."

"Yeah." Considering her former bag-lady looks, the transformation was indeed remarkable. "Looks like she has the entire country eating out of her hand."

"Did you see that piece in the paper this morning?"

How could he have missed it? The newspaper had been delivered to his palace suite along with breakfast. Emblazoned across the front was a picture of "Princess Carly" and a gushing article about the lovely American with the quick wit and the charming habit of knocking things over. They adored her. She'd thrown herself into the lifestyle, learning Montavian culture and history, perfecting her French. Most of all, she'd proven Luc's innocence. When the press discovered Luc had been in America, falling in love, they were captivated by the romance and quickly withdrew the negative stories.

"She's worked hard to make Luc proud of her."

"I know. I'm so glad she uncovered that count dude's plot to take the crown for himself. If not for her investigation, he might have succeeded." Teddi gave a dramatic shudder. "To this point he'd done a good job of hiding his intent and the money he had diverted into his own war chest."

The crowd around them surged forward. Somewhere in the crush were Carly's family and an awestruck Tina Osborne. Carson spotted the bride and groom surrounded by well-wishers.

"Oooh, hurry," Teddi said, grabbing his arm. "There they go."

She dragged him toward the grand hall's double doors, thrown wide for the upcoming departure. She jumped up and down, waving as the prince and princess swept across the room. Carson rolled his eyes. He had already said his goodbyes and congratulations, but tossing rose petals seemed important to his sister, so he went along.

The bride, dark brown waves flowing beneath a tiara-topped veil, wore a long white gown that shimmered and rustled as she moved through the crowd of people and down the tall steps toward the carriage. Luc, in his royal military uniform, held her elbow, pride and love in every intimate look he cast at his new wife.

White streamers flowed out from the carriage. A team of six white beribboned horses, black and silver harness jingling, awaited. The newlyweds stopped and turned, waving one last time before Luc swept his bride into his arms. To the delighted laughter and popping flashbulbs, he kissed her soundly for the whole world to see.

With rose-tinged cheeks a laughing Carly turned and tossed her bouquet into the crowd. Dozens of excited female arms shot into the air, but the giant mound of pink roses landed right in Teddi's hands.

More flashbulbs popped as the stunned recipient jumped and squealed and waved at Carly. Clearly delighted, the bride returned the wave.

Then, with her bridegroom's assistance, the new princess of Montavia stepped with elegant grace into the carriage.

"Carson," a breathless Teddi said, clutching the bouquet to her chest. "Do you realize what this means?"

"It means you were in the way."

She gave him her oh-ye-of-little-faith look. "No, silly. It means that the harmonic balance of love and work has been restored at the Benedict Ranch."

He glared at her. "I won the bet. We're not changing the name of our ranch."

"We don't have to, brother dear. I talked to Macy this morning and she said the phone was ringing off the hook. Word has spread that our little guest ranch sparked a marriage between a prince and a private eye. Singles will come from everywhere in hopes of finding their own true love." She pointed in the direction of the royal carriage. "Singles will come, Carson. They most assuredly will come."

Carson's usual stubborn reaction would have been protest. But in truth, he was pleased with the outcome. Pleased for his friend. Pleased with the increased business at the ranch.

"So I guess we both won the bet, huh?" he said.

"Looks that way." She whacked him on the chest with the bouquet and grinned. "And whether you admit it or not, Carson, love is always a good thing."

Amidst the noise and crush of well-wishers, the royal carriage began to roll down the cobblestone streets. Luc leaned forward and stared straight at Carson. With a wide smile he signaled thumbs-up and mouthed his thanks. And then Prince Luc draped his bride's veil over his head, and the couple disappeared into an ocean of white and the congratulatory shouts of a happy kingdom.

Even a cynic like Carson had to smile.

Yes, indeed. Love *was* a good thing.

* * * * *

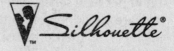

COMING NEXT MONTH

#1814 THAT OLD FEELING—Cara Colter

Accustomed to taking risks, Brandy King wants to bolt when
her father asks her to help widower Clint McPherson through his
emotional turmoil. Now this daredevil woman faces her greatest
challenge—how to handle all the old feelings when she's reunited
with this man who once broke her young heart....

#1815 SOMETHING'S GOTTA GIVE—Teresa Southwick

The weird phone calls and mysterious pop-up messages shook
Jamie Gibson. But her new bodyguard has her definitely on edge.
Sexy, dedicated Sam Brimstone has promised to keep her safe and
then be gone. But trapped between the intense attraction she feels
for Sam and the threat of an unknown stalker, Jamie knows that
something's gotta give....

#1816 SISTER SWAP—Lilian Darcy

Can identical twins really swap places? Singer Roxanna Madison
tries to adopt some of her sister's meeker characteristics for an
important business trip to Italy. But her new boss, the gorgeous
Gino di Bartelli, and his motherless child have her own heart and
voice threatening to bubble to the surface.

#1817 MADE-TO-ORDER WIFE—Judith McWilliams

Billionaire Max Sheridan had assumed the etiquette expert he hired
would be a dowdy grandmother. Instead, the beautifully dynamic
Jessie Martinelli has his orderly mind turning from politeness to
more, well, complicated matters of the heart. Is this expert about
to give him a lesson in love?

SRCNM0406